FOSTER MARY

FOSTER MARY

by Celia Strang

McGraw-Hill Book Company

New York   St. Louis   San Francisco

Library of Congress Cataloging in Publication Data

*Strang, Celia.   Foster Mary.
Summary: Mary's dreams for her foster children
include a warm house, regular meals,
and no more traveling. [1. Foster home care—Fiction.
2. Migrant labor—Fiction] I. Title.
PZ7.S89729Fo   [Fic]   78-23630
ISBN 0-07-061996-4*

Designed by Suzanne Haldane

1 2 3 4 5 6 7 8 9 M U M U 7 8 3 2 1 0 9

For Tommy, Sis, and Andy, who remember Apricot Hill

FOSTER MARY

1 The season was over, the apples all picked. I stood by the irrigation ditch across from the boss's house, my hand on Markheim's head, and watched the old cars going down from Ransome's in a steady stream. The pickers had all been paid off. The locals, from Yakima and other places in the valley, had gone by about half an hour ago, speeding toward the county road. Now the ones we knew better, the families who had lived in the shacks right here in the orchard, were leaving, and I wondered whether we'd ever see any of them again.

An ancient DeSoto, plastered with stickers, held the Marv Summers bunch, Marv, fat and jolly, and his wife, laughing in the front seat, and the rest in back. I saw his married son and his blond wife and baby, and their other boy, Alf. Alf waved his bandanna at me and I yelled a good-bye to him, trying to see all the stickers and figure out what they said.

Alf is fifteen, too, thin and freckled, not as big as I am. He leaned out and pointed to something, yelling, but I didn't know which sign he meant. Kennedy-Johnson was easy, you saw that everywhere, but I didn't know who Boykin was. Under that sign it said, "Everything Is Made For Love," and in still bigger letters, "ALABAMA!" Wow, they were really a long ways from home. Most of the people we traveled with were from Arkansas or Missouri, like us.

These folks took a little longer to load up and get out than the ones from the valley and most of them hoped to leave Yakima far behind before they had to stop for the night. Some would probably spell each other off and keep right on driving south until they got to the California fields.

"How come, Aunt Foster Mary?" Bennie asked last night. "How come we ain't packin' like the rest?" I knew why he wondered; Uncle Alonzo usually burns up the roads trying to get to the next place before all the best jobs are taken, and Auntie likes to do that, too, because she says sometimes the early birds get the good shacks. But sometimes there ain't any good ones, really.

Aunt Foster Mary swept a wisp of gray-brown hair from her forehead and kept on scrubbing, her short arms going up and down on the board like piston rods, her pink face shining from the steam.

She said, "Well, don't say nothing to the folks around here, but I'm just waitin' until Old Lars heads for the

2

asparagus like he says he's goin' to. Then I'm goin' to have Uncle ask for the caretaker's job."

Bennie nodded his dark head and went off to play with the Fennerminger kids for the last time, but I said, "No fear, Lars'll go, all right. He knows he only held on to that job because Mr. Ransome was too busy durin' pickin' to look for anybody better. Uncle might as well go see him now before somebody else does."

"No, that ain't right. We'll wait."

I knew she would say that. No use arguin' with Auntie on a matter where you could say one side was wrong; she had her own ideas and you couldn't budge her. I remembered another steady job Uncle had lost out on, though, and I don't think he even knew how disappointed she was, she never said a word. Still, I had a feeling she had really counted on settling down and staying that time. I can't even remember the name of the little California town where Alonzo heard about that construction job. I only remember that she didn't smile quite so much that night and she was slow with the packing.

A couple of years ago there was another time when he'd been pretty sure he'd get an overseer's job. He would have been good at it, too, but I guess the boss thought he couldn't figure fast enough. Sometimes Alonzo gives you the notion that he's slower than molasses in January, and lots of people might get that mixed up with bein' stupid or lazy. He ain't either one. I've worked right along with him and I've seen him cut more asparagus, pick more apples, or pound more nails than anybody else in the crew. He don't appear to be going fast, he just never stops, that's all, and when the day's over he's earned his money and then some.

I walked past the caretaker's house down the dirt road

to the shacks. The last car was the Fennermingers', full of little towheads. They waved but our Amiella and Bennie were off someplace. Auntie was standing in the door of our cabin and she waved back. Markheim and I walked over.

"That old car don't look like it's even goin' to make it to Yakima, does it?" I could see she was already worryin' about where all them young'uns were going to spend the night.

She said, "Bud, supper's all ready to put on the table. Go find the kids, will you?"

I whistled for Markheim, but he'd left me and gone home to the Ransomes'. I would sure miss that dog if we had to leave. I like German Shepherds better than any other dog. I like them almost better than people.

First I covered the part of the apple orchard where the little ones were allowed to go and then I climbed Apricot Hill, where they weren't, but I couldn't find them. Up on top I looked way out over the valley toward the Mill-housers' ranch and the river and thought how strange it was to be staying after the picking was over.

I thought about how many years it had been. I had actually been born somewhere on the road between Missouri, where my mother's folks lived, and Medford, down in Oregon, where we go most years because the apple season begins earlier there than it does in Washington.

All I could remember, my whole life, was staying a few months in one place and then moving on to the next, although everything else had sure been different since the Meekins had taken me in.

"How come your shack always looks so much better

than the rest?" Mrs. Fennerminger asked once when she came over to borrow some margarine.

I hadn't ever thought about it before, but she was right. It wasn't that Auntie was so awful neat, it was just that she had a way of making a home out of any old place. She made things bright and pretty. Cinnamon applesauce would be bubbling on the stove, a piece of colored oilcloth on the table, a handful of wildflowers in a glass on the one windowsill. Our clean jeans hung on a metal contraption behind the stove. The little kids liked to bring home pictures from school because Aunt Foster Mary saved every one and arranged them on the wall by the window.

"Don't you think he has real talent?" she asked Mrs. Fennerminger, showing her the picture of Bennie's stiff little farmer patting the brown horse. There'd be an apple tree, heavy with fruit, and a dog or a red hen or a cat under the tree. The picture was always about the same things.

Bennie was eight but wherever he went they'd usually put him in the first grade, even though he is big for his age, because he hadn't learned to read yet. I'm fifteen and still in the eighth grade, so I know how he feels.

"What do you like best about school, Bennie?" I asked him, and creasing his forehead like he always did, thinking about it, he told me he liked making a picture to bring home to Auntie. I didn't say so, but the thing I liked best was coming home.

Teachers tried to treat us apple pickers like the rest of the kids, I guess, but you couldn't blame them for not being crazy about having their rooms crowded with kids who were miles behind the rest in every subject. And, of course, they knew we'd be gone at the end of the season, so they never really got to know us. Maybe some of them could have helped us in time but they never had a chance. We didn't stay anywhere long enough.

Amiella is in kindergarten, a funny little five-year-old. I hoped she'd do better in school than us boys did. She loved to bring home flower pictures to put up on the wall. Aunt Foster Mary is crazy about flowers. Alonzo never fails to dig up a little patch of ground for her to plant, though, like us, the flowers don't usually do too well. We never stay in one place long enough for anything to come to full flowering.

I called the kids again and started down the hill, still thinking about Aunt Foster Mary but kind of worrying about where Ben and Amiella were, too.

In the six years I've lived with Auntie and Alonzo the other things I used to know have sort of faded from my mind. Now and then, though, if I see a little kid who looks lost or hungry or afraid of everything, then I know that could have been me, age nine. That's when Alonzo came and got me. My mother had been dead a long time then and my father was drinking so much he couldn't even get on at Elrickson's where the shacks were leaky and had smelly holes and the pay was the poorest in the state. Alonzo found me alone, late at night, waiting for my pa to come home with something to eat. Alonzo just left him a note telling what route we'd be traveling that year, in case he wanted to come and see me. He never came, my old man, and I knew he wouldn't. I never missed him.

Sometimes I sort of remember my mother. "A saint on earth," Aunt Foster Mary used to say of her, and maybe she was, but I know Bennie's wasn't, or Amiella's, either. Just the same, I knew why she said that about each of our mothers, and told us how they loved us. If a kid thinks his own mother hasn't any use for him, how can he have any use for himself?

"How about mine?" Amiella liked to ask, and Auntie would gather her up in her arms and say, "Oh, honey-lamb, I just wisht I had a picture of your mommy to show you! She was a sight for sore eyes, sure enough!"

She would hold the skinny little girl off and look at her and say, " 'Twouldn't surprise me none at all if you turned out to be the spittin' image of her, either. You get more beautiful every day. You even walk that graceful-like way she did. She loved to dance, you know." A look of sorrow would come on her face as she gazed at Amiella and she'd say, softly, "When your Mama passed on, the mourners in that funeral parlor filled the biggest chapel and the little one, too, and the line went clear down past Hayes' Drug Store."

About then she'd start rocking and Amiella would put her blond head on Aunt Foster Mary's big, comfortable bosom, knowing well the words that would come next.

"She always said," my aunt would murmur, "if anything ever happens to me, Mary Meekin, I want you to have my little girl."

Amiella's eyes would be closed by now.

Aunt Foster Mary breathed softly, "I told her, 'Don't you worry, Angel, I'll take her home with me and I'll keep her forever; Alonzo and me, we'll guard her with our very lives.' "

Of that whole flowery speech the only words that were true were the ones about Angel Daniels loving to dance, and that Alonzo and Aunt Foster Mary would surely guard her child with their very lives.

Auntie would be worrying about those kids right now. I had to find them fast and get them home to supper. I called and called and then went on down the hill, looking over across the valley to see all the stripped orchards of peach and apple and cherry as I went.

All of a sudden I thought of something. Up to this time I hadn't much cared whether Uncle got the job or not. I was used to taking things the way they came, and, except for school, not worrying much. But now I looked at those orchards and I thought how in all my years of being a fruit-picker's kid I had never seen the trees in bloom. They must be really a sight in the spring.

I drew a deep breath and crossed my fingers, and I thought, Just once to get to stay in the same place all year, to go to the same school. It might be kind of nice.

When I had almost reached the bottom of the hill I looked toward the rows of shacks, ours the only one showing a curl of smoke from the chimney pipe. I thought I saw Amiella's little polka-dot dress disappearing around the corner of the caretaker's cottage. I called but they didn't hear me. That was another place Auntie'd told them to stay away from, but that's where I found them. Amiella's nose was barely up to the sill, Ben's brown head over hers and both of them on tiptoes, trying to see through the kitchen window.

"What's the big idea?" I asked, sternlike, scowling down on them. "How come I got to go all over the Lord's orchard lookin' for you, and you don't even answer?"

Amiella's blue eyes were big and scared.

"Sh! There's somebody in there. He was makin' funny noises, only now he's stopped. Go in and see who it is, Bud. Climb in the window."

8

"I can't do that," I told them. "This here's Mr. Ransome's orchard, and this house is his property. We ain't moved in yet, and maybe we ain't goin' to. Sure not if we get on the wrong side of the boss."

But I bent down and peeked under the edge of the blind. The floor was littered with paper sacks and bread scraps, just like the shiftless ones always left the cabins; only I would've expected a caretaker to be different. I could just imagine my Aunt Foster Mary going away with a mess like that on the floor.

"Can't see a thing. You two are dreamin' again. Come on, now. Auntie'll have a fit if her good supper gets cold waitin' on you."

"I see somethin'. It's a foot. Under the bed." Bennie said it slow and solemn, like he nearly always spoke, trying to keep from lisping, his tongue held back from that empty place in the front of his mouth.

I saw it now, too, and it *was* a foot, not quite hidden by the mattress that was laying crooked on the old springs.

I pushed up the window. He must have got in this way. I climbed over the sill and put one foot on the floor. And then I stopped cold.

"Don't come no further or I'll shoot!" said a squeaky voice from under the bed. I let out a swear word, forgetting the kids. Because I could see enough of him now to realize that he was a pint-sized bandit for sure, but just the same, he wasn't fooling. He had a big old pistol, all right, and it was pointing straight at me.

2 The muscles in the back of my legs were so tight they began to ache but I didn't make another move. I didn't know why this kid was hiding or what he was up to, but I believed he would pull the trigger, all right. This little booby trap was all set to go off.

The minutes just stopped for a while, like the sun had stopped sinking and it would be evening forever. When my heart slowed down a little bit I thought, O.K., if I'm going to die this stupid way, why, go ahead and shoot, you crummy kid. Only I hope Amiella and Ben have sense enough to light out for home and tell Aunt Foster Mary.

The sill was warm from the sun. Behind my back was

Apricot Hill and on the other side, way over, was the beautiful Naches Valley and a river where kids could go swimming and paddle a boat and have fun together. I couldn't see it, but I knew it was there. And in front of me was a room with a bed and a table and a stove. No other signs of life but the scraps left by Old Lars. And a little kid's unblinking eyes looking at me from under that bed.

I was in an awkward position to back out. I knew I couldn't get my leg back over the sill fast enough. I measured the distance and decided that a dive in his direction would be stupid. The bed was too far away.

I felt a small movement next to my hand on the sill. One of the kids was trying to see around me. Without taking my eyes from that gun I spoke low. "Keep out of sight, you hear me? Duck. Go home, *now*."

And I said to the young monster, craning my neck to see his face better, "O.K. if I go home now? If you want this place it's all yours." When he didn't answer, "Who are you, anyway? Won't your folks be lookin' for you? It's suppertime."

"I ain't got no folks. And it's none of your . . ." Aunt Foster Mary would have me out behind the storage sheds with my jeans down, big as I am, if I said words half as bad as the ones that came rolling out from under that bed.

"Shame on you, Lonnie Hastings. You do, too, have folks. Your little brother is in my class." Amiella spoke sternly from my other side. "Come on out and my big brother will take you home."

"Amiella, you go home! You and Bennie beat it right now, do you hear me? I'll deal with this kid. You stay out of sight."

I hoped she would mind me. The Hastings part rang a bell. Now I remembered. They were the ones who left the kids alone and took off for the taverns as soon as the day's picking was over. Old Lars said he didn't think they even fed their kids some nights, before they left, and in the early hours they came back, loud and quarreling.

"Lonnie, put the gun away. I'm not going to hurt you. Lonnie—" When he didn't make a move, "Your folks have gone. You know that?" No answer. "Are they off lookin' for you? Does your Dad know you got his gun?"

"This is *my* gun. And nobody ain't lookin' for me. I ain't got no folks. And that's not my name."

"Oh, well, in that case, come on out. If you ain't hiding from no one what are you doing under that bed? Come home with me and Aunt Foster Mary will give you some supper."

"Hah! I'll bet." The gun was wobbling a bit, but that didn't make me feel any safer, since it was still pointing my way, and the sharp eyes behind it were not wobbling, not a bit.

Around the corner of the house I heard a small noise, like something slapping down on a board. Lonnie heard it, too, and took a look, but quick turned back to me. Then there was the sound of a key in the lock. Bennie had found it, I thought, under the mat on the step in front of the cottage.

"Bennie!" I yelled. "Don't you open that door or I'll beat you within an inch of your life!"

If it was Bennie, he wasn't paying any attention. The door started to swing in. I looked at it and so did Lonnie, and in that second I dived for the top of the bed.

I knew he could shoot me through the mattress of course, and he probably would.

"Mr. Ransome!" Bennie's voice came from the other side of the door. "Lonnie Hastings, he's in your house. And he's got a gun."

What Lonnie's next move was going to be, I'll never know. He shoved his hand from under the bed, the gun pointing toward the door now, and I leaned over and grabbed it. And in that moment, in walked Bennie.

I hauled the young one out and stood him on his feet, the gun in my other hand, aimed at the floor. I grabbed his shoulder. I didn't mean to hurt him, but I wasn't being gentle, either. His face screwed up and all of a sudden he folded on me. There he was on the old linoleum with bread scraps all around him and dirt streaks showing up where they covered the gray-tan of his cheeks. Except for the clean little river lines left by his tears.

"Don't touch that," I said to Bennie, putting the pistol on a shelf and reaching for Lonnie. As easy as I could, I picked him up. He hardly weighed as much as Amiella. I could feel the skinny little ribs sticking out. I looked for some place to sit down and finally put him on the old mattress and sat next to him. I lifted his shirt up, just far enough to see his back. It only took one look. I knew why Lonnie Hastings had run away. And I knew why his folks had taken off in such a hurry.

"Where's Mr. Ransome?" I asked Bennie, looking up at my sober little brother.

"He went to Yakima. Mrs. Ransome, too. In the pickup."

I had to smile, even though my stomach was threaten-

13

ing to come up to meet my tonsils, since I looked at that back. Some people think Bennie is kind of slow in the head. Hah! He hadn't pretended Uncle Alonzo was there, nobody's afraid of Alonzo. He had said the name of the boss, the man who could make you move out, the one who was the law around the orchards. Even Lonnie would know who Mr. Ransome was.

"Thanks, pal," I muttered to him, then I picked Lonnie up. It was impossible to do it without touching him someplace. He let out another string of swear words and I put him on his feet, easylike.

"Maybe it would be better if you try to walk," I told him.

"I ain't going with you!"

"O.K., Lonnie. Where do you want to go?"

He looked around like a little trapped weasel, his eyes wild. "I'll take you," I told him. "I'll take you wherever you want to go, honest. But Aunt Foster Mary, she's goin' to be awful worried if I don't get these kids home to supper, so why don't you come, too?"

"I don't want no supper!"

"Well, do you want to walk over to the shack with me while I deliver the kids to my aunt? Then you can tell me where you want to go."

I kept hold of his hand, though he tried to pull away, and finally he followed along with me. When he stopped, I stopped, but I kept heading in the direction of home.

"You're takin' me to the police station!"

"No, he ain't. He's takin' you to Aunt Foster Mary." Bennie's voice was calm, and the kid looked at him and then came along.

14

Amiella had gone ahead and Auntie was standing there in the doorway, waiting for us. Alonzo, too, his hand on her shoulder.

"Come in, Bud. Come in, Lonnie," he said, his kind gray eyes taking in my young partner's fighting stance, the tear streaks, too.

"I ain't stayin'." But the smells coming through that open door were too much for him. He sank down on the old rock we use for a step. Looked like he was stayin' for a few minutes, anyway.

"I'll dish up." Aunt Foster Mary turned to go in. "Nice to eat outside, ain't it? Everything seems to taste so much better. Anyhow, it's hotter than Dutch love in here. Who wants to eat out in front with Lonnie?"

Amiella was already handing him a bowl of stew and a spoon before I could speak up. She came back with her own and sat down on the ground beside him.

"I love stew. I love it better than anything except chicken, don't you, Lonnie?"

He looked at her out of the corner of his eyes but didn't answer. He was too busy with the food in front of him. Aunt Foster Mary handed me two thick pieces of bread and I took them out. He clutched his bread without looking up and wiped the bowl with it, stuffing almost all of it into his mouth. Amiella looked at him thoughtfully and chewed her bread.

"Let me get you some more," I said, taking the bowl from his tightly curled fingers. His hands hadn't been washed in days. Auntie hadn't reminded any of us to wash tonight, come to think of it.

He ate another big bowl of stew and another hunk of

bread. He ate it fast, without looking up again. But when Bennie carried out a dish of chocolate pudding and put it in his upstretched hands, he just held it there and quietly and thoroughly he gave up his dinner. When he was all through, he laid the dish on the ground, put his head down on his arms and cried.

Aunt Foster Mary had a warm washcloth ready in no time. She lifted Lonnie's chin and gently washed his face and then his hands. She didn't say a word to him and when Amiella began to talk she said, "Sh, honey. You go inside."

Alonzo, quiet, like always, took the washtub down and put it on the kitchen floor. We poured water from the big teakettle in, and then Bennie and I brought cold water from the faucet by the irrigation ditch. When it felt just right to her wrist, Aunt Foster Mary sent Amiella and Bennie out to play and we took off Lonnie's clothes. I had whispered to her during supper about his back. "You can see the marks the belt buckle made," I told her, but she wasn't prepared for what she saw. One thing my aunt can't stand and that's to see a little kid hurt. Lonnie had been hurt bad. She had to leave him for a minute and go and lean up against the table with her back to us. Then she wiped her face off, came back, and picked up the wash-cloth.

"I won't touch you," she said. "I'll just let the warm water run over your shoulders."

Alonzo's hands were clenched tight. He said, "Here, you take this rag and start in on your arms and legs. Put some soap on it."

Lonnie did just like he told him, meek as Moses. All the

starch had gone out of him. Auntie sent me to get a pair of underpants and a T-shirt of Bennie's from the box under the bed.

She told Lonnie to put his arms on a clean towel on the kitchen table. "Now rest your head on your arms," she directed him. "This is going to hurt. It might sting pretty bad. But in the morning it will feel better." He bent his head over and we couldn't see his face, but he didn't make a sound the whole time she was dabbing the ointment on.

"Bud, dump the water, will you, Son? And call the kids in. I'll let them take their baths tomorrow." Her voice was soft, and her hands pulled the T-shirt on as easy as she could. Then she folded down the cover on Amiella's cot and helped Lonnie to get in.

Alonzo drew the bedspread across the middle of the room for a curtain like he did every night. He rubbed his graying hair with his big, knobby hands, then he patted Lonnie's head and smiled at him, and told us good night. A minute later I heard his heavy work shoes drop on the floor. I pulled down the sleeping bags Aunt Foster Mary made for us boys and spread the pad on the floor where we slept.

"Amiella, you can sleep on the foot of our bed tonight. Tomorrow I'll make a new sleeping bag for Lonnie." My aunt turned to us, her eyes shining. "Tomorrow maybe we'll move into the caretaker's cottage! Wouldn't that be wonderful? Another room, and a stove with an oven. Water in the kitchen, so you boys don't have to haul it all the time, and even electric lights! I got a feeling we're going to stay."

I hoped she was right. I looked over at Lonnie. He was

almost asleep. Looked like he was going to stay, too. I wondered how that would work out. First thing I'd do would be to get that gun and give it to Alonzo.

Auntie felt his hair to see if it was dry yet.

"Well, guess I'll go to bed. 'Night, boys." She latched the screen door and turned to leave us, then softly touched his head again. His eyes were closed now. She looked down for a long time. "Don't it beat all, the way it's the boys who always get the curly hair? He's going to be a handsome man, don't you think? Tall, I bet, and dark. And *good*. You can tell just by lookin' at him. A real good, sweet little boy."

3   The late October sun shone nice and bright but the morning air had a good nip to it. Aunt Foster Mary had us up even earlier than usual and right away she started organizing. She dug out clean shirts for everybody, cut off the worn legs of Bennie's old jeans, and handed them to Amiella.

"Here, honey, you and the boys are going to have a little picnic," she said, and Amiella scrambled back behind the curtain in a hurry and put them on.

My aunt gently smeared some more ointment on Lonnie's back. Then she looked at his old clothes doubtfully, and finally put them to soak in the washtub with the clothes we had worn yesterday. She gave Lonnie Bennie's good pair of jeans and hunted up some old ones for Ben. While we dressed she made the bed and had Alonzo take down the bedspread.

"Get on that side," she told him. "I'm going to put it on the bed. It looks a lot better than this one." Alonzo helped her spread it and they smoothed it down. She gave it an extra tug on the outside so it would come far enough over to hide the box of clothes underneath.

By that time the oatmeal was ready and she sat us all down around the old table. I brought in a wooden apple box from outside the door and Aunt Foster Mary put Amiella up on it and gave Lonnie her chair.

Lonnie reached for the bread with one hand and picked up his spoon with the other. Then he looked around. Uncle Alonzo's hands were clasped in front of him and the little kids' heads were bowed. Aunt Foster Mary sat down and he said, "Thank you, Lord, for this food and for our children. Especially do we thank you, Lord, for this new one you have sent us. Amen."

"Amen," the kids echoed, and we all began to eat. Lonnie dipped his spoon at last into his bowl, not taking his eyes off Alonzo.

"Pass Lonnie the brown sugar, Bud," my aunt said. I took it and sprinkled some on his cereal, but he didn't notice. He was looking around the table now, at the kids busy eating, at Aunt Foster Mary stirring her coffee and, finally, back at Alonzo. His face was still flat and without expression, like it was the first time I saw it, peering out from under that bed, but when Alonzo looked his way something passed between them. My uncle nodded and Lonnie's mouth opened and the spoon went in. He was still eating slowly and watching Alonzo when the other kids jumped down.

"Take the young ones over to the side road, Bud," my aunt said. "Empty the trash can there, and set them to work picking up the papers and stuff around the cabins. Take a rake for Bennie. Tell him to do a nice job and to be careful with the rake."

"He will," I said. "Bennie's always careful." I looked at her. "What do you want them to clean up around the cabins for, Auntie?"

"Because we can't clean up the insides yet," she said, reasonably. "Not until Alonzo gets the job."

I took them off, carrying the rake and a cardboard box. "Tell them when they've done around two or three shacks or when they begin to get tired to come back here," she called after me. "Then they can get their lunch and go up on Apricot Hill."

"We can?" asked Amiella, surprised, looking back.

"Yes. Nobody here but us now, and no dogs either. But when you do come back, come quiet. Your uncle and Mr. Ransome might be talking business." And to me she added, "You better come and see if there's anything you can do to help, once you get the kids busy, Son. And comb your hair. Remind me to cut it tonight. It's gettin' awful long."

"O.K.," I told her, but I couldn't figure all this out. That she'd want the kids out of the way I could see, but I didn't think it would take all that many hours. Either Mr. Ransome would say Alonzo could have the job or not. In that case, we'd be a day behind the others on the road to California.

Still and all, I thought, she must be really hoping. We hadn't packed a thing, not a darned thing.

When I got back everything was cleaned up and the dishes done. Aunt Foster Mary was stirring a chocolate mixture and adding some nuts and dry cereal to it.

"Mmm!" I said. "Smells good. What is it?"

"Cookies. The no-bake kind. That's all I can make here with no oven. But just wait until we get in the cottage."

"If."

"Yes. If."

She fixed a box on top of another one to make a little table and put her breadboard on it.

"What's that for?"

"You just sit over here and do your lessons. But when Mr. Ransome starts telling Alonzo the different things he wants done, you write them down, see?"

"Oh. Well, O.K. Is that all?"

"Write down anything important. Alonzo will work his head off if he gets the job, but he forgets things."

"Where is he?" I asked, and she said, "Out in the sheds, I think, checking on supplies for the cabins."

I sat down and she gave me some milk and cookies and I got my school books. I hardly ever did my homework until Sunday night and then only if she reminded me to, but I started trying to read a chapter in Social Studies and pretty soon my uncle came in.

"Lots of white paint," he told her. "Some green and brown. Quite a bit of rough lumber."

She nodded and handed him a comb. He smiled at her and passed it through his graying hair a couple of times. She took a brush and he stood up again while she got his work pants brushed off for him. He brushed at his shirt a little bit.

"Don't know how I got all this stuff on me," he said, but like his mind was still way off with some other problem.

"You look fine."

Just then we heard steps outside and someone knocked. My aunt opened the screen door and said, "Morning, Mr. Ransome. Come in, why don't you?"

The boss is a nice-looking man, quite a lot taller than Alonzo.

"Fine day," he said. He smiled at her and sat down at the table. She poured him a cup of coffee and one for Alonzo and put the cookies in the middle of the table. Alonzo smiled and sat, too, but didn't say a word.

Mr. Ransome took a bite and said, "Thank you, these are good. Well, Alonzo, Mrs. Meekin tells me you are interested in the caretaker's job."

Alonzo nodded his head. Nobody spoke for a minute or two.

We heard Mrs. Ransome calling her husband. I went to the door. "He's over here!" I yelled. She went back home. "I think she said you were wanted on the phone," I told him.

"Thanks," he answered, and hurried off toward his house.

We waited and waited but he didn't come back. I took a little walk down the road and a car passed me and then stopped in front of Ransome's. A man and woman and a girl with long black hair got out and went up to the door. I went home and told Alonzo the boss had company.

He said, sounding tired, "I got a little work to do on the

car. Call me if he comes back, Mary." He went out by the shed and Aunt Foster Mary kept on moving around the room, quieter than usual. I did my school work.

The kids came and got their lunch. She had it all packed and she smiled at them and waved good-bye when they raced off to climb Apricot Hill. I went out back to help Alonzo.

He was really giving that old car a going-over. Looked like he expected to hit the road again.

" 'Bout time to eat," I told him after a while. I'd been handing him tools and trying to help but he acted like he forgot anyone was there. He was under the car now. I heard him grunt something about a dad-blamed crank-shaft. He slid out in a few minutes and wiped his hands on an old rag. We went into the cabin. I looked around to see if Aunt Foster Mary had been packing, but she was just washing clothes and hanging them on a line Alonzo had strung from the door to a tree. Alonzo and I sat down and ate the lunch she had left laid out on the table.

I wished the kids hadn't gone on this picnic. I was used to their chattering at mealtime. Aunt Foster Mary came in and had a cup of tea, and pretty soon Alonzo went back to his car job. I took a bite of one of those cookies but it didn't seem to taste good like they had this morning.

I was just thinking I'd go and find the kids when they showed up, tired and happy. Lonnie was actually smiling. Amiella's light hair had come loose from the little braid Auntie had made on top of her head and it was floating around like dandelion fluff. She had a long black streak down her face and a tear in the seat of her jeans.

"We slid down the whole mountain!" she yelled. "Way from the top to the bottom!"

"That's no mountain. It's a hill," Bennie told her and then he turned to Aunt Foster Mary, as though apologizing for bringing her home in such a mess. "I told her to slide, Auntie. She said her feet hurt." After a minute he said, "I couldn't carry her. Not downhill."

"Land sakes! I should think not!" my aunt exclaimed, peeling Amiella's clothes off and getting down the washtub again. "Honey, next time don't use all your steam going up, save half of it for the trip home. Either that or try a mountain that ain't so tall."

"Soak a while," Auntie said as she plopped Amiella in. Then to Bennie and Lonnie, "Supper ain't ready, boys. You hungry so soon?"

Lonnie shook his head. "No, I'm just sittin' here, restin'."

"I ate my lunch a long time ago," Ben said. "It was good. But now I'm sort of empty."

"Well, then could be you are hungry again after all that mountain climbin'. So you two have this here bread and butter and I'll hurry up with supper."

"I want a bite, Ben," Amiella piped up, so he broke off exactly half and gave it to her. Lonnie ate all of his.

Alonzo came in. He said, "I been monkeyin' with that drive shaft and I think I got it fixed, but I don't know but what it would be a good idea to take the car over to that service station at the Corners. Bill's a pretty good mechanic and he could put it up on the hoist and take a look at it for me." He turned to Aunt Foster Mary. "I got to buy new tires, anyway. I could see how his compare with the ones in town. I been puttin' it off until we got paid but now I got to buy them."

"How many?" Auntie asked him, and he sighed. "For around here, where I can keep them patched up, if my

spare holds out, two. If we got to go on the road, four."
He wrote something on an envelope. "Ain't this the way it
always goes? You get a little money and there's a dozen
places to put it."

"Well, don't go now, Alonzo. Wait and see." He knew
she meant wait and see if Mr. Ransome comes back, but
he shook his head.

"He just went off with those folks when I came in. Mrs.
Ransome, too. She was all dressed up and so was the boss.
He's forgotten about us."

He got a jacket and said, "I ain't hungry, Mary. I'll have
a bite when I get home."

I went outside when he drove off. It was a nice nippy
fall day, the kind that makes you want to do something,
only I was restless and I didn't know what to do. I
prowled around, wishing I could think of something to
make my aunt and uncle feel better—wishing Mr. Ransome would come back. Did he only come over in the first
place to be polite, because Aunt Foster Mary had spoken
to him about the job? Maybe he never did intend to give it
to Alonzo. Or maybe he figured if Alonzo really wanted a
job, he'd speak out and ask for it himself.

Supper was quiet. The mountain climbers had lost all
their energy and were ready for bed early.

"What's tomorrow?" Amiella asked, rubbing her eyes.

"Sunday, Love," Auntie told her, tucking her in and
looking down at her for a few minutes. Maybe she was
thinking, like I was, that it might be our last day here.

All Sunday morning we wandered around. "He won't
come today, they're never around much on Sunday,"
Alonzo said, but just the same he didn't go very far from
the cabin.

The kids probably wondered what was the matter with this usually noisy family. Lonnie asked if they could go up on the hill again and Auntie said, "Yes. Have a good time. And come home early. We may have to be getting up at the crack of dawn."

"Of course, I know, it's a school day. School days always come after Sunday," Amiella said. She took the bag with the cookies and Bennie and Lonnie took the others after Auntie dropped some crackers and a couple of apples in, and they went racing off. Then it really was quiet around our place.

Nobody had seen hide nor hair of the boss or his wife since they drove by about church time, but now and then Alonzo or Auntie would look out toward the curve in the road, as though they thought they heard somebody coming.

Late in the day we saw the Ransomes come home. Uncle went out back after a while and started in on the car again because Mr. Ransome didn't show up at our place.

I asked Uncle if he needed any help, but he said, "No, Bud. I just want something to do to fill up this blasted afternoon." He was putting the last tire on. They were all new.

"I think you'd better look for them children, Bud," Aunt Foster Mary called from the doorway. "No, wait a bit. Here comes Mr. Ransome."

"Hi. Fine day," he said to her, just like it was yesterday morning. He sat down and I went out back to get Uncle. We came in, Alonzo smiled and sat down, too, and Mr. Ransome said, "When there's a crew working in the orchards, the caretaker would work with them. The rest of the time the job would be mostly maintenance of the cabins, repairs, and so forth, and tending to the irrigation ditches. And letting me know, of course, if an emergency arose."

I turned my back on them and sat at the little table Auntie had fixed up. After a minute I picked up my pencil and tried to concentrate on what he was saying, so I could write it down. Alonzo, of course, wasn't saying a thing. Well, here we go again, I thought.

I looked over my shoulder and he was frowning.

Mr. Ransome said, "I'm renting our house, didn't you know? Probably to Mr. Harrington, the high-school science teacher. He's been anxious to look at it but I haven't had time to talk anything but apples. I told him to wait until the picking was over. So he came out yesterday."

Alonzo still didn't seem to think that those remarks needed any answer on his part. Aunt Foster Mary said, "Mrs. Ransome was telling me one day when I went over to iron for her that you were wanting to move to town."

Mr. Ransome sighed and then smiled a little. "Yes, she thinks it's too lonesome out here now that the children are grown and moved away. She's been looking around for a house in town ever since she knew we'd have a good harvest this year. And a few days ago she found one she really liked, out near the clubhouse. But I guess for me it will mean getting up a lot earlier and getting home later." He added, "And probably not being here when any problems come up."

Alonzo nodded, sympathetically.

Mr. Ransome went on, "I told Mr. Harrington that if he took the place, we'd take care of the yard, so one of the caretaker's jobs would be to keep the grass mowed in my yard, in front of the cottage, and down to the irrigation ditches."

Alonzo nodded and I wrote down, "Mow grass."

"How are you at gardening—flowers, I mean?"

At last Alonzo opened his mouth. He spoke the truth. "Nothin' extra, I guess."

Aunt Mary spoke up. "But I am. I really love to do flower beds."

Alonzo said, "She sure does. I'll take good care of the grass and hedges and do any digging that needs to be done. Bud could help her with the weeding."

Aunt Foster Mary smiled at him for making such a long speech, and waited for him to go on, so he said, "I'm quite a hand at carpentering."

Mr. Ransome's eyes lit up. "Good! I'm not, and the cabins are in pretty bad shape this year."

Aunt Foster Mary spoke again. "You get the best pickers if you got the best places to stay."

"You might be right. We sure didn't get the best ones this year. Some of them were pretty shiftless. Well, I'd like to hear your ideas on what can be done to improve these cabins. I don't want them all to flock to Millhouser's or Lawrence's and leave me with the no-goods next fall."

He stood up and said to Alonzo, "Let's go take a look around. I can't do everything this year, not with buying a new house and all, but maybe we can patch up the worst ones."

There was a loud wail outside. "What's that?" cried Alonzo. He ran out and we followed him. Somebody was hurt. The kids weren't in sight yet, but it sounded like

Lonnie. It was. They came out of the trees, Bennie holding him up on one side, Amiella patting his arm on the other side, and Lonnie limping and crying.

They all spoke at once. "It was an old bee!" Amiella cried, indignantly.

"He stepped on it. On the bee." This from Bennie.

"He stung me! Right on my foot! That old—" We all knew what was coming but Aunt Foster Mary was the quickest. She grabbed him up and hustled him out to the irrigation ditch, his mouth pressed firmly against her shoulder. Whatever swear words rolled out, and I bet they were really something, she managed to stifle them. Loudly she soothed him, and quickly she slapped mud all over his foot.

He struggled desperately and finally she had to let him breathe.

"Not that one!" Lonnie shrieked, sticking out his left foot, now completely covered with a pillow of rich, chocolate earth. "This one!"

So Aunt Foster Mary performed the same operation over again on the other foot, all the time making soothing noises, while his sobs gradually let up.

When she walked back toward us, we all smiled to see the mud on her clean apron and the streak on her face where she had brushed her hair back, but she wasn't paying any attention to us.

"Poor lamb! It'll be better soon," she said, looking down at him tenderly.

Mr. Ransome gave him a little pat.

"What's your name, young fellow? I don't remember this one," he said to Aunt Foster Mary. "I thought you had three."

"No, we have four," she answered. "His name's Lonnie. And when his folks named him after his Uncle Alonzo, they must have known what they were doing, because he gets more like him every day of his life!"

She walked past us and I held the screen door open for them.

"How about a cookie?" She smiled down at Lonnie. "Cookies are a sure cure for bee stings."

4 Mr. Ransome looked at his watch and said, "Didn't know it was so late. Wife's expecting me for dinner. Well, evening, folks, see you tomorrow." He went off toward the big house and I saw Markheim bounding up the road to meet him.

Alonzo didn't seem to know for sure whether he had the job or not. Auntie asked me what I thought and I had to say I didn't know, either.

Uncle worked some more on the car. Aunt Foster Mary fed the kids, washed them up, and put them to bed early. I wandered around, trying to help Alonzo, but he said, "I'm just tinkerin', Son. Go see if Mary needs you." So I knew he wanted to be alone, and I went back inside.

Auntie was washing clothes again. She had the bed-spread hung so that the light from the lantern didn't bother the little kids, asleep over in the corner of the room. I went after more water for rinsing, she added hot from the teakettle and started dunking the clothes but wouldn't let me finish the job.

"I can do it," she said. "Nice and quiet around here, ain't it, now that everyone's gone? I can't hardly ever remember us being the last workers left in an orchard, can you?"

I shook my head. If you asked me, it was a little *too* quiet around here. I told her I was going to take a walk.

"That's a good idea," she said. I went down toward Ransome's and just on an off-chance, gave a whistle when I got to their hedge. I heard Markheim bark and sure enough he came bounding around the far end to meet me.

"Good boy! Good old boy!" I told him, laughing and hanging on to his head to keep him from licking my chin clear up into my hair.

Well, if this did turn out to be our last night here, I thought, Alonzo would be sure to have the car in good running order, Auntie would have every dud we owned nice and clean, and I'd have one more chance to roam the orchards with my best friend. Markheim and I headed for Apricot Hill.

School was a lot quieter the next day, too. There were vacant seats in all the classrooms, and in Miss McCarthy's all the tablet armchairs that had been crowded around the sides, in front of the blackboards, and under the bulletin boards had already been moved out. The picker kids were gone. Now there was plenty of room for the well-dressed children of the ranchers, the not-quite-so-well-dressed town kids, and the few Mexicans whose parents had year-round jobs in this district.

I looked around the room again before Miss McCarthy started talking about Language Arts, and saw a familiar blond head bent over a book. Liz Holbrook. So all the pickers weren't gone, after all. Well, that seat would probably be vacant tomorrow, too, and maybe mine.

I wanted to ask her how come she was still here, but Liz went up to talk to the teacher after class. I waited a few minutes and then left. She was probably telling Miss McCarthy good-bye.

At home things looked just the same. Nothing had been packed. Lonnie and Ben got some bread and apple butter and went outside to play.

Amiella was on her knees beside the bed, carefully putting little pieces of cloth and ribbon into a wooden cigar box that Alonzo had given her.

"What you doing, honey?" I asked her. She wound a strip around a clothespin doll and laid her in the box, too, then said, "Packin'. My child and me, we're movin' today."

"Oh, yeah? Where you movin' to?"

"Caretaker's cottage. Got a nice stove. Going to make cookies every day. My child does love cookies."

"Her and me both. Make some for me, too, will you?"

I looked out and saw Aunt Foster Mary walking up the road. I went to meet her.

"Hi, love," she said. "I been helping Mrs. Ransome a bit." And before I could ask it she answered my question. "Uncle's off with the boss."

34

"They been talkin' all *day?*"

"No, this morning he sent Alonzo to borrow some stuff from Mr. Millhouser. When Alonzo got back Mr. Ransome needed the pickup himself for some errand or other. They didn't go off to look at the cabins until about a half hour ago."

I nodded. Maybe everything was all right. Or maybe the boss had decided by now that Uncle wasn't the man for the job. After Old Lars he probably wanted to be extra careful. I just wished that Alonzo had a chance to show him, had just a week to prove what he could do.

An hour went by. I said to Aunt Foster Mary, "They've been gone a long time. Reckon I ought to go and kind of see what they're doing?"

"No, I guess not. We'll know when we see Alonzo's face. I'll know when I see him walkin' toward us, far as that goes. You know, Bud, it's for Alonzo's sake, as much as for you kids, that we just got to settle down somewhere. He ain't getting any younger, and I worry about that arthritis cripplin' him up, one of these days, if he don't start to take things a little easier."

"You think this is going to be an easy job?"

"No, maybe not. But he'll have a warm house to come back to at night and regular meals, and no more of that travelin' every few months. Seems like we've spent half our lives on the road. Always goin' someplace, and never gettin' anywhere." She looked around the little shack. "Everything we own is right here, in plain sight. Not much, is it?"

I didn't know what to say. I never heard my aunt talk that way before. I swallowed and opened my mouth but

35

before I could think of anything that would make her feel better, her eyes crinkled up and she smiled at me as she walked over to the door and then looked out at the two little boys playing marbles in the shade of an old lilac bush. She turned and looked at Amiella, and at me again, and she said, "Plain sight. Everything that makes life any good at all, it's here, or it will be, when Alonzo gets back. And if he ain't walkin' so springy, why we'll know it ain't God's will after all that we stay here, so we'll pack and tomorrow we'll be on our way."

She looked out the door again. I thought at first she was watching for Alonzo and Mr. Ransome but her eyes were focusing on something far away across the trees as she said, quietlike, "In all this country, all of it that I ever seen, I don't know as there is another spot as pretty as this valley. I could call it home, couldn't you?"

"Yeah. I really like it."

After a few minutes I said, "Auntie, you reckon Mr. Ransome is telling Alonzo a million things he wants done to them shacks? And you reckon Alonzo is just nodding his head and agreeing?"

"Probably. I hope to goodness he don't forget them all before he gets back here. Likely I should have sent you along, after all." She looked in the box she used for a cupboard. "Wonder what we should have for supper? I was kind of thinkin' that we'd go in to Yakima. We're about out of groceries. But I don't know, if we're leavin' tomorrow—" Her voice trailed away. She turned and came back to the door just as I said, clearing my throat and hearing my voice come out husky anyway, "We ain't. We're stayin'. Least I think so." I went over to stand beside her and put my hand on her shoulder. "Look." I crossed my fingers.

She moved closer and together we watched the two men walk slowly toward us and then, without looking our way, turn and go out back toward the storage sheds.

Her shoulders shook and for a minute I thought she was crying. Then I grinned. Once again we were thinking the same thing at the same time. I slapped her on the back and we both howled as I said, "Who did it look like to you? Who was doin' all the talking?"

It was crazy, but we couldn't stop laughing to save our lives. We held on to each other while Amiella came and watched, her eyes big and round.

"Who did it?" she asked politely.

We both answered, "Uncle Alonzo! He was talkin' a mile a minute!"

By the time Mr. Ransome and Uncle Alonzo had finished their confab, Aunt Foster Mary had whisked the two boys in, made them wash, change their shirts, and she had put a clean dress on Amiella and brushed her hair. She held on to the braid she had made on top of Amiella's head and was reaching down in the cigar box on the floor for a ribbon to tie it when Alonzo came inside.

"Ouch!" cried Amiella at the same time that Alonzo spoke from the doorway.

"Well, I got the job."

We all looked at him and smiled and smiled.

"Of course you did," Aunt Foster Mary said fondly. "I never had the slightest doubt that you'd talk him into it."

Alonzo got all red in the face. He leaned over to tie his shoe and said, "He gave me an advance on supplies I'll be needin'. I got to go into Yakima to buy some things. Want to come along?"

"Why, I guess so. I guess we might as well." She winked at us. "You kids want to go to town with your uncle?"

"Yippee!" they yelled and headed for the car.

"Well, now, wait a minute," Alonzo said. "I got to wash up a bit. Get me a clean shirt, will you, Mary?"

He turned and looked at us sternly while he soaped his arms at the sink. "And you wash up, too. Wash good, you boys, behind your ears and everything."

Aunt Foster Mary held a clean blue shirt out and he stuck his hands in the sleeves and smiled at us all. "Because after I buy some nails and tar paper and stuff and we get the groceries, I might take you out to eat. How about that? Where do you want to go?"

"Hot Dog Hut!"

"Hamburgers!"

"Chow mein!"

"Wait a minute, now. One at a time. We'll let Lonnie decide. Sounds to me like he's the only one in the bunch that's got any manners. He ain't said a word." He bent down on one knee and put his hands on Lonnie's shoulders. "Son," he said. "You decide. What are you goin' to order, hm?"

Lonnie wriggled, embarrassed by the attention. Finally he said something low to Uncle Alonzo.

Alonzo nodded, buttoning his shirt and tucking it in before he took Lonnie's hand and started for the door.

"Here's a young feller who knows what he wants," he said, and when we all asked, "What?" he answered seriously, "Hamburgers. Hot dogs. And chow mein."

38

I followed them out to the car. Aunt Foster Mary looked happy, clutching her old purse and hanging on to Amiella with the other hand. The two boys looked happy, already fighting about who'd sit next to the window in the back seat. And Uncle Alonzo, walking around the car, checking the tires before we started, had a smile on his face, too.

I couldn't help thinking what a difference the last few hours had made. How could you *know* it was going to be better? I guessed it would be all right, if they thought so, but some things would be the same. Like school. At least, when you were traveling to a new place, for a little while, the days that you were on the road, you could think maybe this time it'll be different. Maybe in this school I'll know as much as the other kids. Maybe school will be fun.

I looked down and my fingers were still crossed.

5 Uncle Alonzo stopped the car in front of the caretaker's cottage and told us kids to stay where we were. Then he changed his mind and said, "Bud, you come, too."

When I got in there he had a tape measure in his hand and was on his knees in the corner of the kitchen. "Hold this, Son," he said, so I did, while he went to the end of the room. He looked up.

"Mr. Ransome said that before I did any work on the cabins I should fix up our place so it would be comfortable for the winter," he told me, but all the time he was looking at Aunt Foster Mary. "I don't believe your aunt has had a corner she could call her own for a long, long time," he said. "I aim to make this a real home if I can do it. The boss told me that we would have to do something about this floor. He noticed it was full of awful worn spots even before old Lars moved in."

Aunt Mary looked at the floor like it was covered with gold dust instead of bread scraps. After he measured the room across the other way, he did the same thing in the front room. She took the tape measure and started going along the window frames. They both wrote numbers down on an envelope, only he kept right on talking, and she kept right on looking around that little old house like it was a palace and she had just been elected queen. I had never heard Alonzo run off at the mouth like that before, and I had never seen her so quiet. She didn't say one word until he started out the door. Then she went over and stood looking out the back way for quite a while. Alonzo waited for her.

"What would he say, do you think, if you wanted to build a little lean-to right outside this door?" she asked him.

"Good idea," he agreed, nodding his head. "He'd think so, too, I'm sure. I'll ask him. The winters are cold here; that would cut off the wind that sweeps down the canyon. Save on fuel." He looked out the door and measured the distance with his eyes. "Be a good place to put our cut wood. The boys could line it all along the wall of the lean-to and you'd never have to go out in the cold to get it." He put his hand on her shoulder. "It's been hard going these last years, hasn't it, Girl? I never aimed to give you that kind of life."

"I've had a good life," she said, comfortably. "What I'm thinking is that it's time we settled down so the kids could get more schooling than we had. They're smart kids and I want them to go to college."

"College!" I shrieked. "Aunt Foster Mary, you listen to me. If I get through Junior High it'll be a big thing. Don't go thinkin' up any pipe dreams like college, leastways not for Bennie and me. We just haven't got it."

"Wallace Robert Meekin," she said coldly, "I am acquainted real good with my children. I know their faults and I know their strong points. And if you or Benjamin or any kid in this family is lacking any brains, I'd know it before your teachers. What you are weak in is the ability to see yourself the way other folks see you." She fixed me with a fierce eye. "Do you know what's the big trouble with this world today?"

"No. What?"

"Waste, that's what!" she declared. "Americans waste food, they waste everything. Why, just the other day I saw the hired man at Johnson's feeding good apples and number 1 potatoes to the hogs! He said that was the way the government wanted it. Now I'm not going to get myself all in a lather over foolishness like that—it'd be a waste of energy, *but*"— she jutted out her chin and picked up her worn old purse from the chair—"if you think, for one minute, that *I'm* taking part in this sinful way of livin', you've got another thing comin'!" As she started for the door her last words sailed over her shoulder at us, "*And* I'm not aimin' to waste any bright two or three-hundred-I.Q.'d kids on the packin' houses for life, neither!"

42

I shrugged my shoulders at Uncle Alonzo and followed her.

We were all excited about this trip. Everyone knew it was different from a weekly grocery-shopping deal. In Yakima we got the groceries out of the way in nothing flat. Aunt Foster Mary sent me flying in one direction for beans and Alonzo in another for bananas and cabbage. She told Amiella to decide what kind of cookies she wanted, it might be the last package of store-boughten cookies we'd ever taste. She sent Bennie to get a package of weiners and she picked out some fresh meat. Then she grabbed some macaroni and rice and a couple of cans of grits and hurried us to the checkstand. The whole thing hadn't taken us much more than ten minutes.

The food went in the back of the car and we went to the hardware stores and to Sears. Aunt Foster Mary wouldn't let Alonzo buy anything until we covered them all, checking prices, checking quality, checking trade names. At last she was satisfied and they started to buy. Alonzo asked her if she liked the flowery pattern in a linoleum rug they had been thinking about and she said yes, but to hold off on that and get the rest of the stuff he needed—she wanted to take another look around. I went with her down the next aisle where there was a tall pile of squares, all different colors, marked way down.

"How come?" I asked her. "They are a lot cheaper than those on the shelf, and they look exactly the same."

"Probably just a few left in each color. Or maybe they just marked them down to get people into the store to look at floor coverings. I was thinking that if we kept our eyes open for bargains in the squares, by the time that winter came on and Alonzo was ready to do the inside work, we might have enough to do several of the cabin floors."

"Yes," I told her doubtfully, "but they wouldn't match, would they? How would you know if you were going to come out with the right number in each color?"

"I thought just use a border of the colored ones, or even put them hit or miss, and finish with these light ones even if they aren't on sale." She nodded her head. "I'm going to try it in our house and I'm going to tell Alonzo to get all he can of the ones that are marked down."

So we drove off toward home with a lot of linoleum squares and some cans of goopy stuff to put them on with, besides all the nails and other things Alonzo had bought. And Aunt Foster Mary kept peeking in a bag and admiring some cloth she had got for curtains.

"They will look awful good with our new floor," she told Alonzo, contentedly.

"I thought we were going to get something to eat?" Lonnie suddenly asked. He had been a real good kid the whole afternoon but now he was hungry.

"We're stopping at the drive-in on the way home," I told him and he went back to some game he was playing with Bennie where he counted cows and Bennie counted all the horses we passed.

"What are you counting, hon?" I asked Amiella and she said, "Owls. But I haven't seen any yet. Help me, Bud."

Bennie turned his head and spoke to her. "Not owls. Don't choose owls. That's silly."

"But I like owls!" she wailed. "Why is it silly?"

"Because you have to go to bed. At night. And that's when owls come out." She wrinkled up her brows at him and he explained, kindly, "They are nocturnal creatures. Owls are."

Aunt Foster Mary turned and looked at me. Her eyebrows went up and I knew what she meant.

I could have been wrong about Bennie, I told her silently, but not me. I ain't about to go to college.

6   The weeks went on, still bright and pretty, but they sure weren't warm. Winter was in the air and I didn't know if I'd like it or not.

Yesterday Aunt Mary said to Alonzo, "Take them kids when you go for the groceries. Buy them some good shoes. I got to stay home and rustle up something for them all to wear to school."

The new shoes felt funny on my feet. Bennie and Lonnie said theirs felt awful stiff, too. Amiella was the only one who liked shoes better than bare feet.

Thursday morning while we waited out in front of the cottage for Uncle Alonzo to bring the car around, my little sis walked up and down, all the time looking at them.

"I love them, I love them," she sang, "and I know my

teacher will love them, too. They are the prettiest brown shoes I ever seen in my whole life. I ain't never going without shoes again, and when I get rich I'm going to have fourteen pairs."

Just then a big moving van turned the corner of the road and drove up to the Ransomes' house. A man jumped out and went up to the door. The dog came out and barked; Mrs. Ransome came outside and told Markheim to shut up. I was sure goin' to miss that dog.

Mr. Ransome came out and called to Uncle Alonzo, who was driving around from the sheds. Uncle called back that he wouldn't be more than a few minutes, he was just taking us to meet the school bus.

"We would have to go to school today," Lonnie said with a disgusted look on his face. "I should have said I was five instead of six, then I wouldn't of had to go this year, anyway."

"Yes, you would, you'd of had to go to kindergarten with me," Amiella giggled. "Are you really six, Lonnie? You're awful little."

"I'm really seven, if you want to know, missy. And don't get smart"— he stuck his face up close to hers— "or I will take your nose"— he put out his hand and she jumped back— "and I will twist it off your ugly, freckled face, you hear me?"

I stepped over, but Bennie beat me to it. His chin was less than an inch away from Lonnie's.

Lonnie retreated. Bennie came on. "I was kidding," Lonnie muttered. "You know I wouldn't hurt her."

Bennie still advanced. Lonnie fell against the car door Uncle Alonzo had opened. He scrambled inside, and I thought it was a good idea to climb in next. Amiella and Bennie got in the front with Uncle Alonzo.

"Gonna snow today," my uncle observed, squinting at the gray sky. "Good thing we took you to town last night for them shoes." He looked down at Ben's boots. "Comfortable?"

"Well, they're nice and warm," he said, cautiously. "I'll get used to wearing them, I guess."

"Like yours, hon?" He smiled at Amiella and she snuggled up to him.

"I love them, Uncle 'Lonzo. I love them half as much as I do you, and almost as much as I do Bud and Bennie and Lonnie."

"Don't you dare love me!" Lonnie glowered at her. "I don't love no girls at all, and I don't want no girls loving me, you hear? If you even speak to me on the lousy playground, I'll—"

I grinned at him. "Say, 'Hi, Amiella?' or 'Run along now, kiddo?' But you wouldn't be twisting her nose, though, would you?" I put my face up to his, like Bennie had, and he turned his head and looked out the window. After a while I patted him on the shoulder. "We like you, sport, we really do. When things get bad and you get real mad at everything, you can fight me, if you want to. But you got to be awful nice to Amiella if you want to sit down to supper with us instead of eatin' out in back."

I waited. Pretty soon he sneaked a look at me over his shoulder. "You treat her right, get that? There'll be no nose twistin'."

He grunted something and slid down in the seat with his hands in his pockets but he knew I meant what I said.

48

We got to the main road and there were some more kids waiting for the bus so we hadn't missed it, no such luck. Emily Millhouser, whose dad owns the orchards right down Lawrence Road, where we worked last year, nodded to me, and Amiella's little friend Susie something-or-other squealed when she saw the new shoes. Bennie even said "Hi" to two boys, but poor Lonnie, he still didn't seem to know anybody and if he kept that look on his face, he never would.

Uncle waved and drove off. Bennie sighed. I knew he wished he could be home and see the Ransomes move and maybe run errands for Uncle Alonzo and Mr. Ransome. He loved the weekends and I liked them a lot better myself, but if you got to go to school, you got to go to school, so no use beefing. The bus came and we rode to school.

I took Amiella down to the basement and this time she stopped and said, "Wait for me, Bud," and left me in front of the little girls' lavatory while she ran inside. I moved down the hall a ways and she came right back out with a paper towel in her hand. She bent down and carefully wiped off her new shoes. "How do they look?" she asked anxiously. "Oh, fine," I said. "Real good."

She ran back in to get rid of the towel and when she came out, she put her hand in mine and smiled up at me. She said, "The first time I ever had to leave the room by myself—the first day of school—I forgot which place the teacher had taken us to. I was little, then, and I couldn't read, you know, and I went in the wrong one. *That* one. It says BOYS on the door instead of GIRLS." She paused. "The boys' lavatory is a lot different."

I cleared my throat. "That so?"

"Yep. The boys' is painted green. Ours is white, all over." We got to the kindergarten door and I took a look inside. Kids were playing already with big blocks, building a bridge or something. A little bitty girl was sitting in a rocking chair in the corner, rocking a doll, and another one was sweeping the floor with a little broom. Some boys pushed cars and trains around on tracks made of wood and made zooming noises with airplanes. It sure looked nice and uncomplicated down here, for everybody but the teacher. She was pretty good-looking, sort of middling-young, but already she had a kind of frazzled look on her face. She was trying to get the boys up off the floor and into a circle of little chairs but they didn't want to. Just the same, she smiled and looked when Amiella stuck her foot out proudly. I'll be darned if the boys didn't stop playing when she told them to this time, and when she pointed at my sis they all sang, "Amy's got new shoes, new shoes, new shoes. Amy's got some new shoes, she wore to school today." Embarrassing, you'd think, now wouldn't you? But no, Amiella loved it, she ate it up. I waved good-bye and she grinned at me and blew me a kiss and nobody was looking, so I blew one back at her and went off to the salt mines.

I been going to this consolidated school since September first, no, since late in August, almost three months now. They start early here so they can take what they call an "apple vacation," a week or so off when the orchard owners get desperate to get the apples off the trees in time to beat the frost. They really can use the bigger kids then so we all pitch in. Even then, they don't always make it. I remember other years how Alonzo used to get me out of bed when the temperature went way down, and I'd follow along behind him and the orchard owner through the dark and quiet rows of trees, helping them start the little stoves. Seemed like playing God, I always thought, trying to heat a room with a cold floor and no walls or ceilings. Yet, behind this night, when the trees were almost ready to harvest, were all those months of pruning, of irrigating, of spraying, of careful labor. You put your heart's blood into your orchard, Alonzo used to tell us, all your prayers and all your cash, and when you got this far you began to think you had it made, and then, wham! One night the temperature would start going down and on the radio you'd hear the frost warnings at thirty degrees, and at twenty-nine you started cussing or praying, whatever your nature was, and at twenty-eight you went around lighting all the smudge-pots. I never found out what Mr. Ransome was really thinking, but this happened once this year, too, and he never said a word except to direct us in our work, but the lines were deep beside his mouth before the night was over.

Anyway, I been going to this school all fall. Aunt Foster Mary always sees to it that we get registered in time for the beginning of school if we can possibly make it up here from Oklahoma on our old worn-out tires, but just the same, the light ain't even beginning to dawn about all this book stuff. You'd think it would get a little easier as time goes on. Aunt Foster Mary says to have patience, it will; but I tell you by the time apple vacation came in October, I felt like I had been in jail and the warden had asked me wouldn't I like to step out and get a little fresh air for maybe a week? I say, Yes, sir! and I think I'd sooner pull up every stalk of all the asparagus growing under them trees than to open another book before I had to.

Well, apple vacation was long gone, so I had to. First I went to Math and it wasn't easy, though I kind of take to numbers. I don't mean talkin' about them, I mean using them, like how many boxes I'd already picked that day, and if I'd worked two-and-a-half hours so far and could pick at the same rate the rest of the day, how much money would I make before dark at so much a box? That kind is right up my alley but this teacher, Mr. Whitehouse, he's an old fellow, and the way he talks about numbers, you'd think it was a foreign language, or something. First he put a number on the board, and I missed the thing he said next, while my heart was sinking, and then he wrote something else and said, with a kind of scowl, "Find the square root." Now, when they want to find the square of a number that looks just as round as the rest, or when they want me to figure out what X equals without giving me enough information to really cooperate, I give up. I mean, is it going to be any use to me? I say no, but the teachers and Aunt Foster Mary say learn it anyway, and of course, they got me coming and going. I have to put in the time.

Somehow or other, I got through that class. Then I went to Language Arts. What that Miss McCarthy asks us to do to a sentence is way beyond reason. I got in real trouble there, because I had forgotten to do a page she had given us the other day. Mine had nothing on it but my name and the sentences, all about appositives and antecedents and stuff like that. So I got another page to do besides the one I already hadn't done. That was for makeup, she told me.

I really listened and tried to find out what it was all about. I wrote down what she said, but afterward it didn't mean a thing when I read it. I also wrote down "Liz Holbrook" because she was in class that day and one thing I did find out was that Liz knew what the teacher was talking about. I wondered where she'd been the last couple of weeks: I'd been sure she'd gone south.

On the way out of the room, I followed her and when we got on the stairway I jiggled her elbow, and she turned and looked at me. She grinned and we both said at the same time, "How come you're still here?"

She answered first, "Ma got a job in the packing house, maybe for the winter. My old man went on to California. But I caught an awful cold—not used to winter, I guess. Missed a lot of school."

Then she asked, "How about you?"

I tried not to show how proud I was of Alonzo when I answered, "Uncle, he's going to be Mr. Ransome's caretaker this winter. We got tired of movin' all the time, too."

"Yeah. I know what you mean. Sure gets cold here, though."

"That's what I hear. Where you livin'?"

"Old Bluebird Motel, right now, where we were during the season. We got our eyes peeled for a better place though, after payday. See you, Bud."

"Yeah." She was gone to her next class and I hadn't even had a chance to ask her how come she knew so much about all that Language stuff.

It was a long old day and when I met Bennie in the yard waiting for the school bus I saw it had been the same way with him. Poor Bennie, he's such a good, patient little kid.

I know he wouldn't cause the teacher any trouble if he could help it, but then, let's face it, he's such a slow-learning type he probably wouldn't bring any joy into her life, either. Then I remembered what Aunt Foster Mary had said that time, the day we got the cottage. One of us was wrong about Bennie. I thought it was Aunt Foster Mary, even though in most things she was way ahead of the rest of us. She only went through the fourth grade down South, before her folks put her out to work, while Alonzo made it through the sixth, but it's easy enough to see who's the smartest one in our family.

"Can I quit school, Uncle?" I asked Alonzo once, and he rumpled up my hair and said, "Boy, you know I'd like to have your help. I get slower every year. But your aunt would never see it our way. And the law says you got to go, anyway."

So that was that.

Bennie and I hung around, the bus came and still Lonnie hadn't come out. As the last kid climbed on, he tore around the corner of the building, scrambled on, and shoved in next to us.

"Hafta stay after school?" Bennie asked, and he meant well but Lonnie balled up his fists and got ready to punch him. I moved between them and said, "Cool off." He wouldn't talk. I tried to find out what was the matter, but he was just on a slow boil, so we left him alone.

We got off at our corner and the snow began to drift down in big, lazy flakes. By the time we'd walked a mile it was really coming—soft, white globs that stuck to your eyelashes and tasted good on your tongue. It wasn't the first time I'd seen snow, but a fruit-picker's kid sure don't see it often. And even around Yakima they don't often see snow this early.

Lonnie was slogging along next to me and the mad, cantankerous look was all gone from his face, erased by the clean, soft snow.

"In all my life," he said, not looking at me but out over the trees, softly piling up, each little black twig getting a coating of vanilla ice cream, "in my whole life I ain't never seen what they call a White Christmas. Aunt Foster Mary she was tellin' me about how people go on sleigh rides and about the fun we'd have this winter. She said there was a place where we could go tobogganin' clean down Apricot Hill."

"Yeah," I told him. "And we can have a tree and all that stuff. And presents."

He looked at me to see if I was fooling, decided I wasn't, and kicked a stone out of the way, thinking.

"I ain't never gave anybody a present," he said. "And nobody ain't ever given me one, really."

"Well, this year's gonna be different. Aunt Foster Mary and Uncle Alonzo, they set great store by Christmas. Last year we was down in California and we had a real crummy place to stay. We was moving in a couple days anyway, but we sure had a fine old Christmas. We went out to eat at one of those Mexican places, then we found a dime store that was open and everything was marked way down. Uncle Alonzo gave each of us kids a dollar and we spent it for anything we wanted."

"I got a dollar," said Lonnie, softly. "I'm gonna spend it all on one big present." He waited to see what I'd say. I didn't know what to answer. If he really did have a dollar, which I didn't believe, I could just figure who he'd buy that present for, and I didn't blame him either. Poor kid had never had anything in his whole, measly little life.

"I don't know will I buy her a big bottle of perfume or a new dress, or what," he said, "but it'll be pretty. I'm going to get Aunt Foster Mary the fanciest present she ever got in her whole, whole life."

7   Alonzo hollered to me as we were rounding the corner by the cottage, so I dumped my books, took off my good flannel shirt I had been wearing for a coat, and hung it behind the stove to dry. I put another old scroungy one on to work in and hustled out to the storage sheds. He was looking at a whole pile of old furniture and other stuff.

"What's this?" I asked him and he said, "Mr. Ransome told me to get rid of it. It's stuff his wife won't have in her fancy new house. He said to give it to the Salvation Army or haul it to the dump. Thing is, I got to get it out of the way pretty fast because there's a load of lumber and stuff coming I'll be needing for the cabins, and this is the best place to put it. Might come tomorrow, even. Looks to me like your aunt could use some of this, don't you think?"

"Guess so. How you going to haul the rest to the dump or whatever?"

"He rode into town in the moving van with the last load just a few minutes ago. Left the pickup for me. Said his wife would be needing him tomorrow, getting things settled, so I could use it till day after tomorrow. We'll have to let our work on the cottage go for a bit and get this out of the way."

He scratched his head. "Gosh, we got no room to put it in the house while we're still workin' on the floor and all that. Hard enough to be livin' there. We probably should have stayed in the shack until we finished our repairs."

I smiled at that. It would have taken the National Guard itself to keep Aunt Foster Mary from moving her family into that house once she knew it was hers. She had gone through it in a whirlwind of scrubbing, scraping, spraying, and sweeping, made beds, put her kids down, and said, "Good night, all. When you leave for school tomorrow, I'll have a chance to really get this place cleaned up." And she'd been working ever since.

"Why don't I go get her?" I asked him. "The things she wants to keep we could put in that first cabin. It's got a better roof than some and they'd stay dry, I think. Then we could load the rest in the pickup after supper and you could drive it to the dump tomorrow. That way, the shed here would be cleared for your lumber."

He looked relieved. Alonzo likes to have somebody make up his mind for him.

Aunt Foster Mary came on the run and was she happy

to see all that old stuff from the Ransomes' house. I could see there would be mighty little that she wouldn't try to patch up somehow, so while she was thanking the Lord for an old, broken-down sofa and showing Alonzo a barrel of worn clothes and rags, I just got Lonnie and Bennie and put them to work.

"Here, kids," I told them. "You move everything that isn't too heavy for you and I'll take the big stuff. Pile them up way over against the wall of the cabin."

"This is fun," Lonnie said. They tugged and strained and made huffing and puffing noises like they were real moving men and quite a bit of stuff got moved before supper.

When we went inside I looked all around at our little house. Aunt Foster Mary, I knew, was no gladder than the rest of us that Alonzo had landed such a good job. It sure was beginning to look fine in here. I couldn't help but think how awful hard it would be when the day came that we had to leave and go on the road again.

The little kids were shivering; it was really cold these nights. My aunt poured them each a cup of hot cocoa, and rubbed their red hands.

"I got to make you some mittens," she mourned. "I'll unravel one of those old sweaters in the barrel and start knitting right away. Why didn't I have Alonzo get some yarn when he bought you your shoes last night? I declare, it's been so long since I've known what winter was like it's just caught me clean unprepared."

We had already forgotten the cold by that time. Aunt Foster Mary's hopes in that good stove had really been on the mark. It was warm in the little cottage and when she opened the oven door and took out a big pan of baked beans, the smell started my mouth watering.

On her bread board were three loaves, brown and crusty. The coffee can she used for a cookie jar was full, too, I knew without looking. When my uncle said the blessing, it seemed to me that even Lonnie said, "Amen," loud and clear, like he really meant it.

The little kids went to bed soon after supper. Aunt Foster Mary thought it was too cold for them to go out again without coats. She found a couple of extra shirts for Alonzo and me and we worked so hard and moved so fast that we really didn't feel the chill too bad, with a good warm supper inside of us, but we were glad to finish.

"Where did all this stuff come from, anyway?" I asked Alonzo, and he said, "Mostly from their basement. Folks with a house that size are always buying something new and the old one goes downstairs, out of sight. It's lucky for us he didn't get around to taking it to the dump a long time ago."

He turned out the light in the shed and we were on the way to the cottage when we saw my aunt framed in the light from the open door, coming toward us with an old shawl around her shoulders.

"Could you put the lamp on in the shack again?" She sounded like she was apologizing, and we grinned as she explained, "I just now thought of it. I forgot a couple of things." So we went with her to the cabin where the stuff was stored and Alonzo lit the kerosene lamp.

"My! There's a lot, ain't there?" and she looked around, admiring the neat piles we had made. She looked a little ashamed as she pointed to the sofa and said, "Would it be an awful lot of trouble to bring it in tonight?"

"No, no trouble," Alonzo answered. "I only moved it three times already today. What's one more? But I warn you, Woman, you got tomorrow and that's all to make up your mind about what you don't want to keep. I ain't going to ask the boss can I borrow his pickup to go to the dump some time next month."

"I need it all," she said, meekly.

"You ain't got room in our cottage for a whole lot of stuff."

"I know, but some of it we can use to fix up the cabins. Some of those folks haven't got nothing. Repaired a bit, this bench would make a good extra seat. And this old hammock, some little kids would sure enjoy playing in it, if the tears were all mended. I got some ideas about next year, to make it easier for the mothers who pick. I'll tell you later, when I get it all thought out."

While we lifted the sofa she rummaged in the barrel, separating an old red sweater and some rags from the rest.

We hurried as fast as we could, setting the sofa down outside in the snow while we turned off the light and closed the door carefully against all of her treasures. Aunt Foster Mary and I both had a lot of faith in Alonzo's ability to mend anything mendable. I could see she felt we had really struck it rich today. I wondered if Mrs. Ransome, in her beautiful new house out by the country club, was half as happy as my aunt, with a shackful of cast-off stuff from her basement.

She looked a little bit sad, though, when we got inside and were sitting at the table with a bowl of soup to warm us up again.

"Alonzo, I didn't think it would get cold so soon. We got to open that box under the bed tomorrow."

He opened his mouth to argue about it, but she said, "We got to, Alonzo. I don't want to, and I know you don't want to either, but there ain't no two ways about it. It's getting colder every day, and we can't wait."

She patted him on the shoulder as she went by and she said, softly, "Anyway, I ain't ever going to forget that you thought of it all by yourself."

But Alonzo shook his head and sighed, and I knew that whatever the big secret was, he figured he had made another mistake.

8 So the next morning Alonzo opened the box.

"You brought them home!" Lonnie gasped. "I thought you were foolin'. You said try them on just for fun. You said, 'I might buy you one like that when I get rich.'"

Alonzo helped him on with the warm new jacket. He smiled at the little boys. "I really played a trick on you, huh?"

Bennie smoothed the soft pile of the lining. "It's the same one. I picked it out. But I didn't know it was mine. Not for real."

"Now, how did you work that, anyway?" I asked my uncle. "I was with you every minute. We were in a big hurry to get out of there after we got the shoes that night. Are the coats the right sizes and everything?"

"Perfect. Plenty big, anyway. They'll be O.K. for next year, too. We were headed for the door, remember? I told you I forgot the baking powder your aunt wanted. You hurried back across the street to get it and I told Bennie and Lonnie they had two minutes to look at stuff in the toy department, and while they were gone, I grabbed a saleslady and told her to shove them coats in a box fast. I just barely got them in the trunk when you came back. Amiella stayed with me, though, and she asked me what I had in the box, but she was so busy watching her new shoes she didn't even listen to what I said."

"I did, too. You said nails."

Everybody laughed. "Sure a big box of nails," my aunt said.

"Well, this was going to be your uncle's Christmas surprise, but the weather turned so cold yesterday he was scared you would catch a bad cold or pneumonia even, so he's giving them to you today. That's your big present—there won't be an awful lot besides the coats. My, you do look beautiful, though. Pull the hoods down far enough to keep the snow out, now. You going to take them, Alonzo?"

"Yep. Get in the pickup. I'll be right out."

"Wow! Mr. Ransome's pickup!" This was sure an exciting day for the boys. They ran out the door.

"I got to take the pickup. I'm returning some stuff to Mr. Millhouser for the Ransomes. Mary, I'm sorry I spent all that money. I was tryin' to figure in my head how much we had left for the rest of the month, and I figured wrong. I thought I had plenty to buy the boys' coats now, and Bud's present and yours next payday. I forgot I paid fifteen dollars down on something. And I forgot to ask how much the coats were. I should have waited until you were with me. I just ain't used to having a few bucks extra."

"You got good value. They are fine coats. Stop worryin', Alonzo. We'll get by, like we always do."

"You want anything from the store? I got to go to the post office, too. I could bring groceries back."

"They are so high in the village. Better tell me how much money you've got left and let me figure out what we really have to have until payday. Then you can go to a bigger market and get it all at once. Bud, here's your shirt. Could you wear this old sweater underneath it, so you don't freeze today? It don't look so good, but it's warm, the sweater."

"Sure. That's fine." I put them both on. Alonzo looked at me kind of mournfullike and I knew he wished he had a new coat for me, too. Far as that went, he needed one himself. Amiella, too, I guess, except that she got picked up every day by one of the parents out our way, or else by Alonzo, so she wasn't out in the cold like the boys were, waiting for the bus, and walking from the main road home. Aunt Foster Mary made her put on two pairs of stockings, an extra undershirt, a warm dress, and a sweater today, besides her regular little blue jacket. She was out by the pickup, walking up and down, when we got there.

"Why didn't you get in, hon?"

She smiled at her feet. "'Cause I like the feel of my new shoes when I walk. I like to wear them all the time." After a bit she added, "Aunt Foster Mary makes me take them off when I go to bed, but she lets me wear them all the rest of the time, though."

That morning a messenger came to my Language class and gave the teacher a note. Miss McCarthy said, "Stop at my desk on your way out, please, Wallace Meekin," so I did, thinking she was going to assign me some more makeup work, but she handed me the note and it said, "Have Wallace report to Mr. Smith's office after school." I looked at Miss McCarthy and said, "Is it because I'm failing in my work?"

She smiled, her brown eyes soft. She had a soft, pretty voice, too. "No, Wallace. It's hard for you, though, isn't it? See me after school some other day, why don't you? Or in the morning, if that's more convenient. And be sure to tell Mr. Smith that you take the bus so that he won't keep you too long. It's an awful day to walk home."

That was a real jolt, her talking like that. I thought I didn't like her because I hated this Language stuff, and here she was talking to me just like I was one of the orchard-owner's kids. I felt real warm inside as I went for the stairs, but kind of in a daze, too. I turned around and headed for the room again. She was writing something on the board, but she turned when I cleared my throat and she raised her eyebrows and smiled at me.

I just said, "Thank you," and I turned and galloped off.

In the middle of my next class I got a sudden idea. I watched the clock and when it was time for the little kids to have lunch, I got excused to leave the room. I hustled down to Bennie's room and asked his teacher if I could speak to him. I didn't want anybody to hear, so I took him out in the hall for a minute.

"Has Lonnie really got a dollar?" I asked him.

"Yup. He has."

"You sure? Or did he just tell you he had one?"

"I saw it. Yesterday. In the morning."

"Where do you think he got it?"

"Don't know. He just showed it to me."

"When was this?"

"Before school. Outside."

I said, "O.K., Ben." Then I thought of something. "Listen, if I'm not out there in time for the bus, ask Bill if he'll wait a minute while you go to the principal's office to get me, will you? Know where it is?"

He smiled. "Yup. Everybody knows that."

I hurried back. When I tried to eat my own lunch, later on, the bread and peanut butter stuck in my throat. I was pretty sure it was Lonnie who was in trouble, and it must be the dollar. I thought about how mad he was last night. I had forgotten that; he gets mad so easy and so often. It wasn't so much that I didn't want Lonnie to get caught. If he had stolen a dollar from some kid, let him take his punishment, but Aunt Foster Mary would hear about it, and that really made me feel bad. After a minute I realized—and I was really surprised to catch myself thinking it—I hoped he *hadn't* stolen it. My gosh, I was beginning to feel the same way about that little stinker that I did about Bennie. Let's face it, I said, there's really a lot of difference between Lonnie Hastings and Bennie Meekin, and there probably always will be.

I worried all afternoon and finally the last bell rang. I got my sweater and shirt and a pile of books from my locker and headed for Mr. Smith's office.

The office secretary said, "Go right in, Wallace. He's expecting you."

Lonnie was there all right, sitting in a chair in front of the desk. Mr. Smith said, "Hello, Wallace. Sit down here, next to your brother, will you?" He pulled a chair around, too, and somehow he didn't look as big and scary there as he had behind his desk. He had a sort of young face when he smiled, but his hair and eyes and the suit he wore were all gray.

He said, "Seems to be a mixup about some money. I tried to phone your folks to find out about it—whether Lonnie came to school with a dollar or not, whether it was supposed to be used for hot lunches, if so—but you don't have a phone, so I thought I'd talk to you and try to get it straightened out. If we can't, I'll have to send for your mother or father."

"Uncle. We live with our aunt and uncle. On Mr. Ransome's ranch." Again I couldn't help sounding proud, "My uncle, he's Mr. Ransome's caretaker."

"I see. Then maybe I could reach him through the Ransomes."

"They've moved to town."

"Oh. Well, this matter should have been settled in Lonnie's room, or in the room of the boy who lost a dollar yesterday, but Lonnie won't talk. He won't help at all and Roland's teacher, Miss Sampson, kind of gave up on him last night. Today she called me in to see if I could find out what really happened." He smiled at Lonnie, but Lonnie just sat there scowling, looking awful little in that big chair, and awful mean, too.

"Now, Lonnie, let's start all over again. Where did you find the dollar? Or did you bring it from home?" He looked over at me, and I shook my head.

"Your brother doesn't seem to think so. Lonnie?"

"Answer Mr. Smith, Lonnie."

But he didn't look at Mr. Smith. He looked at me and he said, "It ain't his. It couldn't be. It ain't that big boy's."

Mr. Smith said, "I told Roland to stay in the outside office. The fur seems to fly between the two of them." He stepped to the door. "Miss Jenkins. Send Roland Forrester in, will you?"

A big, chunky kid about eleven years old walked in and glared at Lonnie.

"That's the kid who's got my money!" he said. Lonnie glared back.

"Sit down, Roland. And let me take care of this, will you, please? Sit over there." Mr. Smith put the big kid as far away as possible.

Miss Jenkins was still in the doorway. "Lonnie's other brother is here, too," she said. "He says the bus driver is going to leave now."

Mr. Smith sighed. "Write a note and send it down to Bill, will you, please? Tell him I won't keep the boys any longer than I have to."

We could hear somebody crying out there. Mr. Smith's eyebrows went up and Miss Jenkins said, "I haven't been able to straighten that problem out yet. It's one of the little Mexican girls. She shakes her head when I ask if she's lost, but—" she raised her shoulders.

He smiled. "I'll be through here in a minute, and come out." He closed the door.

"Now, O.K., Lonnie doesn't want to talk, so let's hear you, Roland. Just the facts, please."

"I laid my wallet down," he brought it out of his pocket,

a nice, brown leather wallet, "and when I went to pick up my books and stuff"—he paused dramatically—"I thought I'd just check, and my dollar was gone!"

It sounded true, and it probably was.

Mr. Smith's voice was kind, though, as he spoke to Lonnie. I guess he just wanted to get the mess out of the way, and us on the bus and out of his hair. "Lonnie, tell me this, did you have a dollar when you came to school Thursday morning?"

I was surprised to hear Lonnie say, "No."

"Then, don't you think this might be Roland's dollar?"

"No, it ain't his."

Mr. Smith sounded like he was getting tired. "Lonnie, did you take the dollar from a purse you found on the playground?"

"No!"

"Did you find a dollar somewhere else on the playground?" At this Roland sneered and said, but not very loud, "He didn't, 'cause it *wasn't* nowhere else."

"I asked *Lonnie*, Roland." Mr. Smith's voice was sharp. Well, he's trying to show that he ain't taking sides, I thought, but I knew Lonnie would catch it just the same, when he owned up.

"Yes, I found it, but it ain't his." Everyone was surprised when Lonnie admitted that much. He was so stubborn I was sure he'd never do it. I looked at him. Then I leaned over and patted him on the shoulder.

"Where did you find it, Lonnie?" I asked him, but he shook his head. "It ain't his," he repeated.

"Tell him. Tell Mr. Smith." I said it firmly. "And hurry up. A busload of kids is waiting for us."

He gave up and looked at Mr. Smith. "It wasn't in no pocketbook," he said desperately, "and it ain't his. It was under the merry-go-round thing that the little kids ride on."

Mr. Smith walked us to the door. "Lonnie," he said, putting his hand on my brother's shoulder, "usually when a thing is found, we say to turn it in to the office. *Somebody* lost it, you know. But you feel pretty strongly about this and I'm not going to *make* you do it. I do not believe you stole this money." Lonnie looked at him, eyes wide open, listening to every word. "I've had a good deal of experience with boys and I can tell when one is telling the truth, I think. Most of the time, anyway." He smiled at us and then turned around to look at Roland. "I've met this boy before. I think I'd like to ask him a few more questions."

We couldn't believe it, a principal siding in with pickers against a well-off town boy like that.

"Good night. Tell Bill I'm very sorry to have disrupted his schedule." Roland was sidling out the door. Mr. Smith said, still politely, "Just a minute, Roland. You don't have to take the bus, do you? Come inside, please."

We said, "Good night," and I hurried down the steps. "Come *on*, Lonnie!" I called back to him. He came, but when we got clear to the bottom he turned toward me like he was going to say something, and then started climbing, one foot after the other, all the way back up those stairs. I went with him, and after I had a look at his face, I didn't say anything else. Whatever it was, he was sure going to do it. On the top step he sat down, undid the laces of one boot and went in with them dangling. When he got to Miss Jenkins he reached down inside his boot, took

71

something out, carefully unfolded it and touched her on the shoulder. She was still kneeling down, talking to the little Mexican girl.

She looked up and he held it out to her and maybe I was the only one there who knew how much it was costing him to give it up.

"Here," he said, "I found it on the playground. I'm turning it in."

"Dólar! Maria's dólar!" A rainbow smile broke out on the little girl's face. "I lose! The papa spank! Gracias!" She grabbed it, and everybody but Lonnie smiled, Miss Jenkins in some relief.

"Where did you lose it, Maria?" she asked, but the child just shook her head and hung on to the dollar.

"Was it to pay for the lunches?"

"Sí! The 'ot lunch!"

Lonnie bent down to her. She beamed at him.

"You were riding on the merry-go-round, weren't you?" She smiled and nodded. "Next time," he said sternly, "you go in and give your money to your teacher, and *then* go riding on the merry-go-round!"

Mr. Smith was still standing in the doorway. He grinned at me.

"You've got a good boy there," he told me.

"That's what my aunt thinks." I grinned back at him. Well, by golly, maybe she was right at that. A real, good, sweet little boy, she said. You can tell just by looking at him. I took a look at him. The tears were running down his face. Maybe they were for the dollar that he had thought he could keep. But on the other hand, maybe they were because somebody liked a little picker kid and knew when he was telling the truth.

9   It really was a terrible day; the teacher was right. I was glad that Bill, the bus driver, waited for us. He was sort of cross about being held up, because the snow was coming down like mad now and the wind was blowing too. The flakes danced and swirled and didn't seem to hit the ground at all. They were fine, each one like a little sharp sword instead of big and soft and lazy the way they looked yesterday.

When we got off I told him, "Thank you," again. He grunted something. I hoped he wouldn't be too late delivering all the other kids just on account of us. Bennie and Lonnie waved at him before he drove away and he tooted his horn at us and waved back, so I guess he wasn't too mad.

The road to Ransome's seemed mighty long to me. I kept my hands in my pants' pockets and my head down, but the little boys chased each other all the way home, shaking the lower branches of the trees to make the snow fall off and aiming snowballs at each other. I thought to myself that most anybody could be happy in the summertime. But winter was another story for poor folks. How come kids like this Roland looked so mean when they had so much? I knew now he'd been lying about the dollar. He probably saw Lonnie show it to Bennie on the playground. How else would he know it was Lonnie who had a dollar? How would he know who to accuse? Mr. Smith saw that right away.

I was gladder to see our house than I'd ever been before. Uncle Alonzo was back at the floor job. He was on his knees carefully laying each little square in place after spreading the goop. He was way over in the far corner now, almost finished. He smiled at us, but I could see his legs hurt as he got up and tried to stand straight.

"Let me finish, Alonzo," I told him. "Just as soon as I get warmed up. I can do that. You take a rest."

"I worked some more on the lean-to today," he said. "Come and see. I got it all done except for some inside work. I thought I'd better do that first, now it's so cold. Already it makes a difference." He opened the back door. It looked dark out there, but I could see he had all the rough work done.

"Yeah, it sure makes the house a lot warmer," I said.

"From now on," Aunt Foster Mary told Bennie and

74

Lonnie, "try to remember to come in this way. You can stamp the snow off your boots out here, see, and brush your clothes off." She was taking a broom to the backs of their new coats. They gave them to her and she hung them behind the stove. Then she looked at me. I was warming my hands, but they hadn't really thawed out yet.

"Try these on," she told me and held out a pair of brown knitted gloves. "I knew you'd need fingers in yours, for helping your uncle work, and handling tools, and like that. Won't take me near as long to do the others. They can have mittens."

"Gee, they sure are nice," I said, admiring them. "How did you know how big to make them?"

"Tried 'em on Alonzo," she said. "Your hands are almost as big as his." She looked at my uncle. "Alonzo, I've been thinkin'. I know I've always fought against debt, but after all, you got a paycheck coming up and this boy is going to catch pneumonia for sure if we don't get him some warm clothes." She stepped around the kitchen, getting the table set. "You were so smart to buy the little boy's coats when you did! I want you to take this kid in town tomorrow, and buy him a coat and another pair of pants, real warm ones, and a sweatshirt, and I'll get busy and knit him a good sweater if you'll bring me some yarn, and I'll make a nice cap for him, too."

"I can wait," I said. "This old sweater under my flannel outside shirt, it helped a lot. Don't charge anything. I know you hate the idea."

She smiled at me and said, "Ever stop to think that poor

folks sometimes take pride in not doin' things they couldn't do anyway? Who'd give credit to a fruit picker? Lots of 'em say they wouldn't take relief money, too. Truth is, they never stay anyplace long enough to be eligible, so they couldn't get it if they wanted it. I ain't proud of one of my children coming home as cold as you are. I'm ashamed."

"I been thinkin', too," said Alonzo, helping Amiella to get up on her chair. "I been hatchin' up a lot of things, I have. Tell you after supper."

"O.K., Uncle 'Lonzo. I'll think of a nice something to tell you, too," Amiella piped up. "I'll tell you after supper, after I finish thinkin' it."

He patted her on top of her blond pigtail that had come undone and was sticking up on top of her head.

"I meant your auntie this time, Little Bug. I ain't going to tell you yet. Not until day after tomorrow."

After supper I helped Alonzo finish the floor. Aunt Foster Mary had been out in the first cabin again and had brought in some more things. While we worked, she examined some of the clothes from the barrel. Some were old things of Mr. Ransome's. "I'm fixing to make a rag rug for next to our bed," she said. "And one for under my sink, and a couple for the boys to put down under their sleeping bags. When you get the lean-to finished we'll let them sleep out there. Then they won't be kept awake while we are busy nights in here."

Alonzo sat back and thought about that. "I could make them bunks to sleep in," he offered. "One long one for Bud on the end wall and double-deckers for Lonnie and Ben."

76

"Where will I sleep? Can I sleep in the lean-to? I want a bunk!" Amiella begged him.

"Nope, the lean-to is going to be the boy's room," Aunt Foster Mary put in. "We are going to keep on putting you to bed in our room at night; then when we get through workin', we'll move you back out here. You'll be sound asleep."

"I'll try to get that sofa fixed next." Alonzo went over and examined it. "I'm going to have to tear it all apart, I guess, and build it over, but I think I can do it. It'll make a good bed for Amiella."

"And someday I'll cover it with some pretty material," said my aunt. "My, what I'd give to be back in Missouri for just a little while!"

Alonzo looked up, startled. "What do you want to be back in Missouri for? I thought you said you'd be happy if you could spend the rest of your days here in the valley?"

"I mean I'd like to use my sister's sewing machine for a spell. Look at this nice old coat of Mrs. Ransome's. Think what a good coat I could make for Amiella out of it if I only had a machine. I'm going to figure something out, I don't know what."

She was looking at the coat, smoothing the soft tan material with her hands, but I happened to take a good look at Alonzo and he had a wide grin on his face. He turned away so she wouldn't see him, but not before he gave me a big wink.

Now what's he up to? I thought. Maybe he's gone and bought a coat for her, too.

We all went to bed early. My feet were on the warm brick Aunt Foster Mary had taken out of the oven for me, and the kitchen was nice and cozy, but I couldn't get to sleep for a long time. They were in the other room now and I heard their voices go on and on, quiet, but like they were talking about something that made them feel good.

The next day I got up slowlike, hating to leave my warm bed for the day that was ahead of me. And I had a big surprise. The sun was streaming through the window like everything. I couldn't believe it!

"Alonzo!" I called, and he and Auntie answered from the front room. I found them at the open front door looking out.

"Jest take a look!" Alonzo said. I did, and saw all the trees dripping, water running into the ditches, the snow disappearing like a spring thaw.

The kids heard us laughing at the sight and came out rubbing their eyes. All except Lonnie: his were wide open.

"Oh, darnit, darnit, anyway!" he cried, really disappointed. "I was gonna build me a snowman today! I ain't never in all my whole life had a chanst to make a snowman!"

"Well, blame your uncle," Auntie said, dryly, but smiling at the gleeful Alonzo. "He's got a special deal on with the weatherman. Tryin' to hold off cold weather till Christmas, but I don't think it's going to work. You'll get your snowman, Lonnie. This is Yakima where we're livin' now."

"All I ask is two weeks," Alonzo said, still smiling. "One more payday."

And I'll be dad-blamed if he didn't make it. The fair weather continued, Auntie found warm shirts to fix up for me and Alonzo from Mr. Ransome's stuff in the big barrel, and whatever the surprise was that they kept whispering about, they didn't let us in on it for quite a while.

But one day when I was walking down the hall from Language Arts with Liz she pointed out the window and said, "Well, I'm sure glad my mom finally got my winter coat paid for. She picked it up last night, and none too soon. We got winter again, Bud."

There they were, those lazy snowflakes, twisting and whirling and coming down like they were going to fall forever.

"Yeah. We sure have," I told her. I still stood there, looking out, when she left me and hurried to her next class.

That night Alonzo was waiting for me with the pickup. He made the kids take the school bus.

"Just Bud, this time," he said. "Your aunt wants you at home. She's got some important things she wants you to do." So we rode off alone toward Yakima.

"Mr. Ransome went into town with Mr. Millhouser to some meeting, and he said for me to keep the pickup. I got some things to get for him at the lumber company," he said, grinning all over.

We picked up the stuff for Mr. Ransome. Alonzo was in a big hurry, though. He could hardly wait to get the stuff loaded, then he hustled me over to the same store where he'd got the boys' coats.

"Your turn now, Son," he said. "'Bout time, too."

Gosh, I was just about as excited as those kids were when they found out he'd really bought the coats.

"This is too expensive," I said. He was urging me to try one on, and I saw the price tag. "I don't need a jacket as good as this one, Alonzo."

But he made me take a real nice, warm jacket, heavy corduroy, with that soft pile kind of lining. I had never had a coat like that before. And we got the other stuff, too. New pants, everything. He gave me a list of things to pick out for Aunt Foster Mary, yarn for my socks and cap and all that. Then he stepped back to the office to arrange about charging them until payday.

I held off on giving the things to the clerk until he came back, but when he did he was smiling and said, "I just told them to call Mr. Ransome, I was his caretaker. No problem. Now come on before the stores close. I got one more thing to pick up, provided I can get a little more credit."

We went to the back of another store and down some stairs to a place where secondhand furniture was stored.

"I came to pick up the sewing machine for Mrs. Meekin," he told a salesman. "I paid fifteen dollars on it the other day, and I'd like to charge the rest until payday."

The man went to get the machine and Alonzo grinned at me. "Your aunt will just about jump out of her skin," he told me. "I think she'd rather have a sewing machine than a Cadillac."

"I thought you had something up your sleeve when she mentioned that machine but I didn't know what it was."

It turned out to be an old one but it was in pretty good shape. Alonzo said he had gone over it carefully.

"I don't know sewing machines," he said, "but I think this is a good buy. Well, I'll sign the paper and you can help me get it out to the truck."

Outside, he said, "Spread this old tarp on top of it. I don't want your aunt to see it yet."

He stopped at a dime store, too, but wouldn't let me come in. He came out with two big bags. It took a long time to get home. We stalled twice on our road.

When we got there the little kids were stringing yards of popcorn and making paper chains all over the kitchen table. They had had supper. I was going to show them my stuff, but Alonzo said, "Not now," so we ate and got ready for bed.

"What did you make today? How come we didn't have it tonight?" I asked my aunt, looking in the cupboard and trying to find what it was that made such a good smell all over the house.

"Never you mind, it ain't for now, Bud. Fix your pads out in the lean-to, will you? Your uncle and I have some work to do and I want the boys to get their sleep."

Lonnie said, "We don't have no school tomorrow on account of the snow! How come we got to go to bed early?"

"Is it early? My, just seems late, I guess. Oh well, you can stay up a little while, then. I'll fix a place on the table for you and you can make some more popcorn strings."

"We got lots of time. Ain't even got a tree, yet."

Alonzo grinned again. He was sure having fun about something.

After a while they got the little kids started to bed. Amiella tried to argue, but she was yawning. Lonnie opened his mouth, too, but Alonzo took him by the hand and led him to the lean-to.

We had left the door open to warm up the little room, but now he closed it and said, "I think we'll have to let Bud in on the big secret, don't you, Mary?" He went on to me, "We decided to celebrate Christmas early, as long as

81

everybody needs their presents right now. While you were in school I got a little tree from the woodlot, now we'll trim it."

"You mean we're going to have Christmas tomorrow?"

"Sure. They'll be home from school. Don't you think it's a good idea?"

"Fine with me. What do you want me to do?"

"Go get the tree, will you? I put it in the first cabin with the rest of the stuff."

So I brought the tree in and we set it up by the front window. We put the popcorn strings and paper chains on and Aunt Foster Mary brought out the goodies she had hidden: cookies in the shape of stars and trees, all decorated with colored frosting, and taffy wrapped up in silver, and fudge pieces covered with wax paper and then pretty, bright-colored stuff.

"Where'd you get all the shiny paper?" I asked her, and she said, "Out of all those magazines Mrs. Ransome left."

The little tree really looked pretty when we had it all covered with the homemade decorations.

"The ones in the big windows in town don't look a mite better, Mary," Alonzo told her. "Now, Bud, get your packages. They'll be no surprise to you, but the little kids ain't seen them, or Mary, either." So I put them under the tree and they told me to go to bed.

Seemed like no time before it was morning. I woke early like always on school mornings and then remembered. I wished I had some money and could have got something nice for Alonzo and for Aunt Foster Mary. Here we all had new clothes and they wouldn't get anything. "Next Christmas I will," I thought to myself. "I'll earn some money and buy them—" I couldn't think what, but I had a long time to figure that out. Anyway, I knew they were happy to have a house and to be able to stay here for a while.

I got up quietlike and stepped over the little kids. My aunt and uncle were already in the kitchen. She was beating up pancake batter and had a frying pan on.

"Don't peek at anything until you get washed and the kids come out," she whispered, so I washed up and called them. Amiella popped out of the bedroom, all dressed, just as the boys came through from the lean-to, rubbing their eyes.

"Merry Christmas!" the three of us yelled, and they woke up fast.

"Is it really?" asked Bennie, his eyes wide, but Lonnie was ready to believe it. "Wow!" he said, softly, when he saw the tree. He walked all around it, just sticking one finger out to touch the pretty decorations. Amiella was on her knees in front of a little dollhouse made of two apple boxes nailed together. Alonzo had painted it and Aunt Foster Mary had put one of the linoleum squares in on one side and a piece of heavy cloth on the other floor for a rug. In one room they had placed a tiny Christmas tree and on the floor near the tree was a baby doll, wrapped in a piece of flannel. There was another doll, too, a little girl, standing up. They were only about three inches high, the kind you get in the dime store, but Amiella sure had stars in her eyes looking at her dollhouse family.

"Didn't have time to make you much furniture," Alonzo told her, "but I will. I'll make beds and tables and everything. Have plenty of time these cold winter nights after supper. You just order the furniture and I'll make it for you."

"Oh, Uncle 'Lonzo, I love it so much!" she said, and stopped to hug him. Then she was back on the floor again, holding the baby doll and showing her the tiny tree.

By this time the boys had discovered packages with their names printed on top, and they were trying to get the strings untied. Uncle Alonzo had bought them each a warm new sweatshirt, like mine, and had made them wooden pencil boxes by putting partitions in cigar boxes. Lonnie's was painted blue and had blue pencils and an eraser; Bennie's was red. They each had a box of crayons and there was another one wrapped up for Amiella.

"Wow!" Lonnie kept saying, his voice getting higher and more excited all the time. Bennie beamed on everybody. They decided to get their clothes on so everybody put on the new shirts. They admired mine, too, and my new pants. We all looked pretty fancy when we were finally ready for breakfast.

"Have you opened everything? Is it time to make the pancakes?" Aunt Foster Mary asked and Bennie said, "No. Here is something else. Starts with A." And he handed it to Amiella.

"Look again," I said. He spelled out A-L-O-N-Z-O, and he and Lonnie both yelled, "Alonzo! It's for you, Uncle Alonzo!"

"Well, I declare." He opened it up and found some gloves like mine and a knitted scarf.

"Good thing I had a little head start on *this* present. I was already making them when Alonzo decided to celebrate Christmas early," Aunt Foster Mary told us, smiling at Alonzo, who had the gloves on and the scarf wound around his neck.

"I'm ready!" he said, sitting down at the table and

84

picking up his fork. Bennie and Amiella screamed at his antics, but I looked at Lonnie and he was standing by Aunt Foster Mary, holding her finger and looking up into her face. For the second time in two weeks this hard-boiled little customer was about to cry.

"What is it, love?" she said, pulling him onto her lap. He struggled with his voice for a minute and then gave up and buried his head in her neck. He sobbed bitterly.

"I think I know," I told them, so the story about the dollar finally came out. "Mr. Smith said he was a good boy," I finished.

She wiped his face and gave him a hug and he said, "I was going to buy a big present for you with the money."

Alonzo said, "Oh, well, *that* dollar's gone and you done the right thing, so don't feel bad. How about the dollars that you and Bennie are going to earn from me next week helping to haul stuff for the cabins? I figured that you might want to buy a present for your aunt and I clean forgot to have you write your own name on the card. See, I only wrote *From your kids and Alonzo*, but we can easy fix that. Just get out one of those new pencils and I'll sharpen it for you and you can each write your name on this here envelope. That's the way it should have been done; I was just too tired last night to think of important things like that."

Lonnie got the pencil and began to smile as Alonzo whispered in his ear. We all wrote our names and then Alonzo said, "Now, I'll need your help, all of you kids. It's a mighty big package. See, this one's from *all* the family and it's the only one Aunt Mary gets, so come with me and we'll haul it in."

Everybody got coats and hats on, even Amiella.

"Don't go 'way, now. We'll be right back," he said to my aunt and we trooped out to the car.

We unloaded the machine, leaving the tarp on top, because the snow was still coming down. He took the front end and I took the back, and we held it so all the kids could lift too. When we got to the door, he said, "O.K., now. Lonnie, you hold the door open! And everybody yell, 'Merry Christmas, Aunt Foster Mary!'"

Lonnie's face was shining with excitement. He threw open the door and we trooped in together, shouting.

She was standing there, her face all pink and smiley, but when Uncle Alonzo threw off the tarp with a flourish and she saw that sewing machine, she had to reach out for the edge of the table and then she sat down. Lonnie jumped around, waiting for her to say something but she couldn't. She just looked at each one of us and then at Alonzo and she reached out and squeezed his hand.

"I think I'll put it over there, under the window," she finally managed, wiping her eyes and blowing her nose. She looked all around the little room and even to me it looked the way I think she saw it, all shiny and beautiful.

"My, I don't know what to say, I'm so trembly. Ain't it a lovely machine? That's one thing apple pickers can't ever have—a sewing machine. Now I really got the feeling that we're staying."

10   Aunt Foster Mary found some paper bags and cut out pieces for the kids to draw on. They started in right after breakfast, making snow pictures and coloring Christmas trees to decorate the wall.

Alonzo worked for a while on the bunks in the lean-to and then fixed the sofa. "Only temporary," he said, "but it will hold up for now."

He sat down to rest and whittled on a piece of wood.

"What is it, Uncle 'Lonzo?" Lonnie wanted to know.

"You wait a few minutes and see if you can guess," Alonzo told him.

"A whistle!" shouted the boys. "Who is it for?"

"This one's Lonnie's. Next one's for you, Ben."

"I am ready to order somethin' for my house," Amiella said, thoughtfully. "I b'lieve I need a bed for the baby most of all. Then a chair for Big Sister to sit in." After a minute she added, "I'll let you know tomorrow what else I need."

"Gosh, I might just as well sit right here and whittle away and never do any work at all," Alonzo told them. "That'd be a fine life, too. Ain't nothin' makes me quite so happy as to have a good solid chunk of wood in one hand and a nice sharp knife in the other."

I chopped some kindling and rustled up a lot of split wood. I piled it along the lean-to wall to help keep the tarpaper up and the room warm until Uncle had time to really finish it off right. We had to dry out some of the wood behind the stove.

The snow kept on coming down. In late afternoon it stopped and we went outside, bundled up warm in our new coats, and we all looked at this white Christmas world. It was like magic, everything changed. There was nobody in sight, not even a car, not a track in the whole big, blanket-covered orchard. You could hardly make out where the road was supposed to be; the snow was clear up on the fence posts.

"Mr. Ransome says that somewhere up in the shed rafters is a big old sled that belonged to his kids when they were little," my uncle told us. "He said you could use it. Maybe I better go find it."

They whooped and hollered at that. Lonnie picked up a hunk of snow and threw it at Bennie.

"Just a minute! Leave us get out of the way before you start a snowball fight," Auntie said. "I better go in and get going on those mittens if you are fixing to have a sledding party."

Alonzo took off his new gloves and put them on Bennie so I gave mine to Lonnie.

"They are a little big," Alonzo said, "but better than nothing, I guess. My gosh! Who's that coming?"

I could hear it too, something chugging and pushing, the sound muffled by the heavy fall of snow. It stopped after a bit, then started wheezing and starting and stopping again.

Alonzo went to the shed and got the wooden snow shovel and we walked down the road to the corner.

It was a truck with our composition roofing stuff and the lumber that Mr. Ransome had said he was going to send out. The truck driver leaned down and handed us some letters for Mr. Ransome and one for Alonzo.

"Mr. Ransome asked me to stop at the mailbox in case you hadn't been able to get up to the road," he said. "I pretty near gave up back there a ways. Is it much farther to the sheds or wherever you want this stuff?"

"Nope, almost there. We'll help." We used the shovel in front of the wheels and he finally got the truck going again. We threw the shovel in back and rode up to the place with him. He unloaded fast and we helped do that, too.

It was nearly dark and I didn't wonder that he was worried about getting back to town.

"Wait a minute!" Alonzo called as he got ready to drive off. "Some of this mail is for the Ransomes. I'll put the new address on it if you'll take it back with you and drop it in the post office in town."

"O.K., but he won't get it for a while, he's gone to California." He took the envelopes after Alonzo had me help him address them right, waved good-bye and drove off.

"Hope he makes it," Alonzo said. "I think he's mixed up about Mr. Ransome, though. When I saw the boss he didn't say anything about going away. If he'd been plannin' that, he'd of come after the pickup, wouldn't he?"

"Don't know," I answered. "Looks like this letter is from him. Come in and read it, why don't you?"

But he turned the light on in the shed, instead.

"Hard for me to read this kind of writin' without my glasses. Can you make it out, Bud?"

It looked like it had been written in a hurry, all right. I squinted at the close-written words and then read:

Dear Alonzo:

My daughter and her family were coming to Yakima to spend Christmas with us but her little girl got sick so we decided to go to see them instead.

No way to get you on the phone and the weather was so bad I thought I wouldn't take the time to come out.

Ordered stuff you wanted. You won't be able to get at the roofs for a while. About the inside work: do the best you can to get the better cabins in shape. Let the worst ones go until the weather clears and I get back.

I think your idea about turning one of the cabins into a combination bathroom with a stall shower is real good. I think we could leave the trash burner stove in to heat the hot water for the present. I checked Sears and you were real close on the prices. Cost of installation is what I'm worrying about. See if you can work out a real close estimate on that.

Enclosed find check. Will drop you a line again later.

If any emergency comes up, call me at my daughter's. Am enclosing her number in San Diego.

Use the pickup all you want. If Joe Millhouser or his boy come over have them show you how to put the snowplow blades on the tractor. You are sure to need it to keep the road open during the worst of this weather.

A little warm sun sounds good to us after this week, so we may stay a while. Not much I could do home anyway. Like I told you, as a carpenter I'm a great orchard man.

Merry Christmas! Am enclosing small check as a remembrance from Mrs. Ransome and me.

His name was scrawled at the bottom of the page. Alonzo folded the two checks and stuck them back in the letter.

"Looks like I have until the New Year, anyway, to show the boss what I can do." He sounded kind of pleased. "Well, you take these in and show Aunt Mary and I'll be along as soon as I find that sled."

He took a big ladder and rested it up against the rafters.

"Let me help you. I'll hold it steady," I said. "Or do you want me to climb up and take a look?"

"No, I think I know where it is. I can do it." He started up the ladder just as Aunt Foster Mary called us for dinner.

I said, "Uncle, let it go until tomorrow, why don't you? It's getting dark. The kids have to go in for supper, anyway." So he came back down. We both headed for the house, hurrying because we were really cold now.

I opened the door and felt the warm rooms welcoming us in. The bowls of food were already in the middle of the table. We smelled hot rolls and chili and string beans with onions and bacon in them. An apple pie cooled on the breadboard. "Wow!" I said, swinging Amiella high in the air to make her scream. "If you cooked this dinner, Sissy, you sure did a fine job! I am so hungry I could take a bite out of anything handy." So I took a big one out of the back of her neck.

"Aunt Foster Mary cooked the dinner," she giggled. "I set the table, though. And I made a decoration for you. We made them for everybody."

"Me, too. I made this one," said Bennie, holding up a small card that was folded so that it would stand up. He had written Uncle Alonzo in neat letters and had made a little tree on it with his new crayons. He set it carefully at the end of the table.

Amiella brought hers over to me. "B-U-D, Bud. That's what it says and I wrote it. Bennie showed me how."

"Mine's no good," gloomed Lonnie, grabbing it from the table. "I can't write, darnit! I can't write at all!" Of course he had taken the longest name and had tried to get Aunt Foster Mary all on one little card.

"Don't throw it away!" She caught him just before he put it in the woodbox. "I love your picture. Look, Bud. See the cute little Santy."

"Here," I told him. "Make her another. Why did you try to write the whole thing? Just write Mary, M-A-R-Y, like this." So he did, and I cut out his Santa.

"I ain't got nothing to make it stay on with!" he bleated.

"Have a stick of gum," Alonzo said, taking one out of his pocket. "Just chew a little. Save the rest for after supper." He handed Lonnie the whole package.

"Is it all for me?"

"I'm givin' it to you, ain't I? Course, there ain't no law against you sharing it with your sister and brothers if you want to."

"You're always givin' me things. Every day you give me something." I looked up in surprise. For Lonnie to be grateful for anything and to say so out loud was a new wrinkle entirely. He was watching Uncle Alonzo. Alonzo picked him up and gave him a hug before he put him in a chair next to his.

"You know something? Every day I'm glad that you came to live with us."

"Yes," said Aunt Foster Mary, admiring her new card. "It was a lucky day for us, the day we found Lonnie. What we needed at our house was another boy."

Everybody gathered around Uncle Alonzo's chair when we had eaten so much we couldn't swallow another bite. He read Mr. Ransome's letter out loud, slowly, pointing at each word with his knotty finger, and peering over his glasses. He showed us the checks. "Sixty-seven," he said, "and another ten for Christmas."

"We got so much to be thankful for." He was folding the sheets carefully, and putting his glasses away, too. "I got this job and this nice little house that goes with it. All a man can really ask for is a good partner," Aunt Foster Mary smiled at him and went on with her knitting, "a bunch of healthy kids, and a chance to earn an honest livin'. You won't be hearin' me complain if I never in my life got more than I got right now."

"I'm thankful, too," my aunt said, unrolling some more red yarn from her ball. "Wasn't it lucky that we decided to celebrate Christmas ahead of time? Way it looks now, it's going to snow until January. Maybe if we'd waited we wouldn't even have been able to get in to Yakima to buy your things. Folks around here say it ain't uncommon some years for schools to close up for several days, account of the buses not bein' able to pick up the kids."

The boys whooped again at this, Amiella too. Then she began to cry, "I wouldn't be able to see my teacher!" she said, and Auntie comforted her. "If we do have a sort of extra holiday on account of snow, you got to make it up spring vacation or in June. You'll see your teacher just as many days. But I kind of doubt if you see much of her this coming week, honey."

"You know what else I'm thankful for?" She turned to Alonzo. "We got plenty of food in the cupboard. We could have been caught short there, too. And I got my sewing machine and I can make my curtains and a coat for Amiella. And I'm so glad for the warm things you bought the kids so they can enjoy the snow."

"Tomorrow Uncle Alonzo's gettin' us out a big sled," put in Lonnie. "It's so big that we can all three ride on it at once. We are goin' sleddin'. How about that?"

"Yeah, how about that?" I said, pretending to glare at him. "How about *me* ridin' on that sled? It's more my size. You'll be lucky if I don't wake up before you do and sneak that sled out of the barn and go clean up on top of Apricot Hill. I know a place where I could ride on my good ol' sled all day and you'd never find me."

Lonnie looked really alarmed at this, but Bennie was grinning, so he decided I was fooling until I told him, standing up and yawning widely, "Tell you what. I'll take it tomorrow and Sunday and you can have it Monday and Tuesday, providin' you don't have to go to school. That's fair, ain't it; two days for me, and two days for you? Big kids first, natch."

Bennie just laughed. "Come on to bed. I'll wake up first. I always wake up before Bud does."

"Ha!" I snorted. "A likely story. I climbed over two bodies this morning and I was all dressed before you even opened your eyes."

"Well, you won't have to climb over anybody tomorrow. Your Uncle's got the bunks for the little boys all fixed. He'll do yours soon." Aunt Foster Mary was rocking Amiella back and forth in her arms.

"Another thing I'm going to do is fix that old busted rocker that the Ransomes left. Just think of you waitin' all this time for a rockin' chair," Alonzo said, kind of sleepy. "Your kids will all be too big to be rocked if I don't hurry up."

I grinned to myself first thing in the morning when I saw the empty bunks. The little kids had eaten and were hustling into their coats and Uncle Alonzo had already gone out to get the sled.

"They didn't give him any peace at all." Aunt Mary smiled at me. "Sit down, Bud, and have some oatmeal."

"I'll go help him get the sled down first. Don't dish up for me yet, Auntie. I'll be right back."

Lonnie and Ben were following me, yelling and cavorting around and making snowballs as they went, tossing them at each other and ducking the ones they got in return. They were better at ducking than throwing; most of the snowballs went wild into the air.

I heard another yell, but it wasn't the boys.

"Shut up, you guys!" I cried. "Keep still a minute, can't you?" They did, but I knew now what I had heard; I knew as sure as if I'd been there, where I should have been, and all the way out to the shed, running as fast as I could, I knew what I'd find when I got there.

11   "Alonzo, oh no, Alonzo, why didn't you call me? Where does it hurt?" I cried, kneeling down by him.

"My leg," he said, his face all screwed up with the pain. "And my ribs, feels like."

"Is it broken?" But I didn't need to ask. I could tell by looking when I eased up his pants leg.

"Bennie! Lonnie!" They were in the doorway, scared and whimpering. "Go get Aunt Foster Mary! Don't cry, now, don't scare her; he ain't dead, you know." They took off like a pair of deer.

I tried to rest his leg on my coat.

"Darn fool, that's what I am! I spent half my life on a

ladder, but this time I guess I was hurryin' and I didn't brace it proper." His face was white and drawn down with pain. I hoped Aunt Foster Mary would come fast. I shut my eyes for a minute, wishing we could live the last fifteen minutes over again and have it come out a different way.

Auntie must have flown. She came in looking pretty white, too, but calm and collected like she always was; and immediately she sized up the situation.

She gently felt his leg, then said, real quiet, "Bud, get me one of those laths. Break it so the pieces are about this long." She measured with her hands. The little hatchet I chop kindling with was right there, so I cut the lath and gave her the pieces. She took off her apron, reached into Alonzo's pocket and got his knife, and cut the seam so the apron would tear. She tore off several strips. Then she carefully put one piece of lath on one side of the leg and one on the other. While I held them, she wound the splints firmly in place. When she had tied the cloth over the splint, she told him to lean back a little more and, with me supporting his back, she felt the ribs, her gentle fingers pressing just a little.

"How did you do this? Did you scrape it on the ladder when you fell?"

"Guess so. I don't really know how I did any of it. I just remember slipping and yelling bloody murder as I went down."

"What I'm wondering is if you got any broken ribs. I think they are just scraped. Seems to me we'd be doin' you less damage to move you inside where you'd be warm than to leave you here on a day like this." She looked at me.

98

"It's going to take time to get help. Even if we're lucky, it's going take a long time with the roads the way they are. What do you think, Bud?"

"I know in an automobile accident they say leave 'em there until the ambulance comes, but . . ."

"Yes, on account of something may have been hurt inside, or a rib might puncture a lung. But look, see the long red scrape mark?" She lifted his flannel shirt and his undershirt. "That's what hurts. I think we could tell if his ribs were broken."

Alonzo said, "Leave me try to move a bit." He straightened the upper part of his body cautiously. "It hurts, but I don't think anything there is busted. I knew my leg was, even before I saw it."

"O.K., let's try it. Bud, take that side, you're taller, and I'll help here. Move him real easy; don't worry about how long it takes." The little boys were still in the doorway, looking solemn. "Bennie, go get Auntie's shawl, will you, love?" Bennie took off without waiting to hear more. "Lonnie, you go see that Amiella stays in where it's warm. And you watch for us at the window. When we get up to the house, open the door, but keep it shut until we come." Lonnie was crying but he nodded and ran off, too.

We raised Uncle carefully and got ourselves fixed, with his arms around our shoulders. I held his right shoulder high.

"Keep that leg up as much as you can," Aunt Foster Mary said. "Does it hurt too much, Alonzo? Try to bear it until we get you inside. If you got pneumonia, too, you would really be in a fix, now wouldn't you?"

She kept on talking to him to get his mind off the pain

but I could tell he was having a hard time just to keep from crying out. He didn't try to answer, but helped us the best he could with his one good leg.

It took a long time to get him inside. We put him in bed with his pillow under his legs and another pillow to keep the covers from pressing on the broken one. She gave him hot tea and some aspirin and then we tried to think what to do next.

"Alonzo," I said, "did Mr. Ransome leave the keys to his house with you?"

"Sure. He's expectin' Mr. Harrington to move in any day now."

"Oh, well. We might not be so bad off then." I was relieved. I got the keys and hurried over there to phone, but I might have known it wouldn't be that easy. The line was dead. He had either had it disconnected or the lines to the main road were down. I hoped they weren't all down because the next place to try was Mr. Millhouser's.

Alonzo was dozing, tired out from the shock and from walking to the house. I sure hated to disturb him.

"I got to," I told my aunt and she nodded.

"Alonzo." I touched him on the shoulder. "Alonzo, I might be able to make it to the road. It ain't snowed much since the truck was here and I could follow in their tracks. I can drive. Give me the keys, Alonzo." So he did.

I knew Alonzo had put antifreeze in our old car and the pickup both, when we went in town. I got the pickup as far as the road in front of our house all right, but it got stuck. The snow started coming down again. The wheels went around and I couldn't make it another foot forward. It was hopeless, but I tried our old car anyway. It stalled before I even got it in front of our house. We never did need chains before, but we sure needed them now. I wished Mr. Ransome had put his snow tires on the pickup; then we might have had a chance.

"Aunt Foster Mary," I called, stamping the snow off my boots in the lean-to. "I'll walk to Millhouser's. Don't worry if it takes a while. Awful hard walkin'. I'll get back as soon as I can."

"First get in here and get in proper shape for a trip like that!" she said. "Set down there and take your boots off." She got a pair of Alonzo's heavy socks and made me put them on over a pair of my own. I pulled my boots on. Then she reminded me that I hadn't had any breakfast and made me eat some hot oatmeal. While I ate she warmed the old sweater to put on under my new jacket. She made me wind Alonzo's scarf around my neck and at the last minute decided that I should wear an extra pair of his pants.

"Besides my own?" I yelped. "You'll have me so loaded down I won't be able to walk at all! I don't need them." I took a look in the bedroom. Alonzo opened his eyes and tried to wink at me. I squeezed his shoulder.

"Find a doc who's a fast worker," he joked. "Give him until New Year's to get me on my feet again." Almost under his breath, so Aunt Foster Mary couldn't hear, he added, "He better be fast if he wants to get paid. If he ain't, I've sure as God made little green apples lost my job." His gray eyes looked out at something 'way off and they had no light in them anymore.

"I'll get the fastest one in town," I told him. I looked back from the doorway and it seemed to me he'd shrunk since yesterday. Just a little man he was now, all the Christmas joy gone, all the plans and all the promises broken in two like the bones of his poor busted leg.

Auntie watched me from the window and her eyes were worried. I picked up a stick, a big tough one, and plodded off, my head way down in my neck to keep the cold wind out of my eyes. I might wander over to the side, but there was the wire fence to keep me from getting lost. The main problem was to make any headway; the wind tried to push me back every time I took a step forward. I sure wished it was blowing from the other direction. I needed to go fast.

I tried to keep in the middle of the road and follow the tracks made by the big truck, but they were hard to see now. The snow fell steady. The stick helped, but it was easier just to pull up the wool scarf and go by feel.

The snowflakes came down soft at first but as the wind blew stronger, they grew harder and sharper, like hail. I could hardly believe this was the same road I walked on every school day almost without thinking about it. Today it took forever.

I was half-frozen when I heard a noise, a soft whooshing sound, and squinted my eyes in that direction. It was a jeep, plowing through the drifts and turning from another side road almost opposite me. Then I realized that I was only a few steps from Lawrence Road and that the county road crew had been by already today. There was only a light fall of snow here.

"Wait!" I yelled, hurrying as fast as I could after the jeep. It seemed like he was stopping; he must have seen me, I thought. I ran to catch up and all of a sudden hit an icy spot. My feet went up in the air and I came down hard on the seat of my pants, all the wind knocked out of me. I stayed there on the ground, trying to wave my hand at the disappearing jeep and hoping he was just hunting for a good place to turn around. When I couldn't see his taillights anymore I started to say all the nasty words I used to hear my father say; I was surprised to find that I remembered him so well. Then I rolled out some that I had picked up from Lonnie and when I got through with those, I made up a few new ones. I thought to myself that even Aunt Foster Mary might not blame me too much.

"Thank your lucky stars you didn't fall in a hole and break *your* leg, boy!" That's what Alonzo would probably say, and I knew it was true, too. The thought of him got me on my feet again and headed down the road toward the Millhousers'. The walking was much easier here, or would have been if my backside hadn't taken such a wallop.

The snow was letting up a little and the lights in their house looked so good to me that I almost cried when I finally saw them. With the kind of luck the Mcekins had had today I'd been prepared to find nobody home at all. I hobbled down their driveway and up the steps. At the first ring, the Millhouser boy opened the door and Emily was right behind him. They brought me in by the fire and got their parents. In about one minute, Mr. Millhouser was on the phone. I can't even remember telling him the whole story; he sure didn't waste any time.

Mrs. Millhouser brought me a cup of hot coffee. Usually I don't like the taste too well, but this was sure good. I drank it without waiting for it to cool off at all.

"Who did you call?" Mrs. Millhouser asked her husband and he said, "Sheriff. He'll know the best thing to do." In a minute the sheriff rang back. Mr. Millhouser said, "Don't worry about that. I'll get the road clear before the ambulance gets here. Just finished using my snowplow on my own place. Blades on, no problem. Thanks a lot, Sheriff."

He pulled his mackinaw on and said, "O.K., Bud." I thanked Mrs. Millhouser and before I knew it we were in the tractor and headed up our road. It had taken me so long to cover that ground on foot, but we made it in a matter of fifteen minutes or so.

Aunt Foster Mary was sure glad to see us. Mr. Millhouser went in to take a look at Alonzo but he seemed to be asleep. He tiptoed back and said, "Glad you've got his feet up and his head down. That's exactly right. I think shock is the thing to watch out for in a case like this. He looks pretty white. Did you give him anything?"

"Just tea and some aspirin. Didn't have anything else."

Mr. Millhouser took a bottle out of his big coat pocket. "Mix a few tablespoons of this whiskey with some hot water and a little sugar," he said.

Auntie had the mixture back in no time. She touched Alonzo on the shoulder and Mr. Millhouser raised him gently while he swallowed some of it. Alonzo nodded to Mr. Millhouser but he didn't try to talk and they put him back down until the ambulance got there. We all sat around the stove talking quietly and worrying about Alonzo.

"I'll be glad to take you in to the hospital. We could stop at my house and get the car. I could bring you home tonight, after the doctor's set his leg, or whatever. I got chains on, but we won't have any trouble getting back now your road's opened up, anyway," Mr. Millhouser told my aunt.

She looked at him gratefully. "I don't know how we can ever thank you or pay you back," she said and he smiled and answered that that's what neighbors are for.

"It's been a long time since we've had what you'd call neighbors, but I'm sure they ain't many like you," she said. Just then we heard the ambulance drive up. Two young men came in with a stretcher. They lifted Alonzo and put him on it, covered him over with blankets and in a minute my uncle was gone.

"Can you take care of the kids all right, Bud?" Aunt Foster Mary asked, pulling on her old coat.

They all hugged her and I said, "You bet. Don't hurry." She looked at me and spoke quietly. "Bud, it's all going to turn out all right. Don't be worrying, I'm not. Now, there's plenty to eat on hand. Bennie, keep the woodbox full. Lonnie, you help Bud figure out what to have for dinner. Amiella," she leaned down to kiss her on the top of the head, "be a good girl."

When we were alone, Amiella said, "Everybody's got a job but me."

"I need you to set the table."

"O.K., I'll do it right now." They all got busy and I tried to figure out what to feed them. Finally we decided on tomato soup and fried egg sandwiches. They seemed to be satisfied. I wasn't very hungry after all. My insides were churning round and round, but I swallowed some food and it wasn't too bad.

It was lonesome as all get-out with my aunt and uncle both gone. I wandered around the little house, not able to settle down to doing anything and I thought for the first time in a good many years about how awful much they meant to me, to all of us.

Amiella had stacked the dishes up on the drainboard and was drawing at the table. "I'm makin' a little tiny picture for my dollhouse wall," she told Lonnie. Bennie was looking out the window, though I'm sure he couldn't see a thing but the snow that was coming down again, quietly now. The wind had finally stopped blowing.

Where would we be, us kids, where would we be today if Alonzo and Aunt Foster Mary hadn't taken us in, I thought to myself. I didn't think Angel Daniels was dead. More likely she had gone to jail for a while. She was a no-good one, I remembered that. Amiella would probably be locked in a furnished room somewhere, waiting for her mother to get home from wherever she'd spent the night.

Bennie was awful quiet. How much did he remember about that run-down Missouri farm where he used to live? I didn't remember too much myself; we were only around that one summer. Alonzo was doing odd jobs on the place, waiting to leave for Medford, where the season was always earlier than in the Yakima Valley. We were camping out in a tent down by the river.

Bennie was a little shaver, not even four, following his mother around and getting slapped every time he got in her way. She had taken a job as a hired girl and you could tell she hated it.

"I got a better job offered me in town as soon as I have this kid," she said, slapping herself in front. "I'll be goin' to the hospital any day now. Miz Meekin, you wanta keep an eye on Ben while I'm gone? I'll pay you with my first paycheck."

Of course Auntie said she would, so when his Ma left for the hospital we took him down to the tent to stay with us. The next thing we knew, a few days after the baby was born, she had skipped town without either Bennie or the baby. We still hadn't heard from her when it was time to leave for Medford to work in the early apples, so we just took Bennie with us and he's been with us ever since.

"What'll we do now, Bud?" asked Amiella, tired of her drawing. The boys looked up at me too. Lonnie's eyes were a little red, I thought. Well, Alonzo and Aunt Foster Mary weren't here, so I had to take their place the best I could.

"How about popping some corn?" I was rummaging in the cupboard and I found a can.

Bennie brightened. He got up and went over to the shelf. "Aunt Foster Mary makes it in this. This old iron frying pan. With the cover on it." He tried to haul it out from the bottom shelf.

"I love popcorn. I love it better'n anything. Can we have cocoa, too?" asked Amiella.

"Oh, I guess so. You'll have to help me, though. I ain't so much when it comes to cooking." I ain't so much when it comes to anything if you want to know the truth, I thought, and once again I wished I had been out there with Alonzo, holding the ladder.

Bennie reached for the can of popcorn at the same time Lonnie grabbed it. Everybody was trying to help at once. Lonnie tried to pour some into the frying pan on the stove and when he felt the steam coming out of the teakettle spout, he yelled, "Ouch!" and dropped the can. The popcorn went all over the floor.

"I never meant to do it!" he yelled, almost in tears.

"I know. It's all right, Lonnie," I told him. "Get me the broom." And as much to myself as to him I said, "No use cryin' over spilled milk."

12 I checked on the kids. Amiella was quiet in the big bed. There wasn't a sound from the lean-to, but I couldn't sleep. I tried to, on the pad on the floor in the lean-to, and on Aunt Foster Mary and Alonzo's bed in the other room. I lay down for a while on the old sofa. Finally about ten o'clock I wound a blanket around my shoulders and sat by the window, waiting. It was so quiet I thought I could hear the snow falling. It was really coming down again. I worried about Mr. Millhouser getting back with Aunt Foster Mary. But most of all, I worried about Alonzo.

I guess I dozed a little bit because I didn't see them come home. The light from the car turning around in front of the cottage woke me up. Mr. Millhouser was headed in the direction of his house when he stopped the car and let Aunt Mary out. He waited until she had opened the door and got inside before he waved and drove off.

She looked awfully tired but she smiled when she saw me.

"Oh, the fire feels good. I thought it would be out. It's getting awfully cold." She took her things off and I said, "Want me to warm you up some cocoa?"

"That would be good."

I pushed the pan to the front of the stove, but the cocoa was all dried up so I put it in the sink and got a clean one out. When the new batch was hot I poured it and brought her a cup. I tasted some, too. It was kind of bitter. I brought the sugar bowl over.

"I'm not so hot as a cook," I apologized. I was worried because her eyes didn't seem to focus on anything and she wasn't talking.

At that she looked at me and turned off the other thoughts, whatever they were.

"Bud," she said, "I don't know what I would ever do without you."

"How's Uncle?"

"He's in good hands. I told Mr. Millhouser we didn't have a doctor, so he called his own, Dr. Lawrence. He belongs to the family they named Lawrence Road after, Mr. Millhouser said. A young doctor, smart. He was so nice to us." She took a deep breath. "First, they gave him a sedative and got him ready for bed. I don't know exactly what they did in the emergency ward before Dr. Lawrence got there, but after he came and examined Alonzo and gave him a pill, he came out in the waiting room and talked to me. He said he has Alonzo scheduled for surgery tomorrow in the morning."

"Surgery? Then he *was* hurt somewhere else? We shouldn't have moved him!"

"No, no. It's just his leg. But it's a compound something and Alonzo ain't young. I can't remember all he said, something about open reduction and something pinning, tibula, I think. He explained about that part. He's going to put a pin in to help the bone to knit. He will be im—" she paused. "It will be a long time before Alonzo can get around again."

"You mean a good many weeks? That'll kill Alonzo."

"More than weeks. Months. It'll probably be a long time before the pin comes out. It ain't going to be easy, the doctor warned me. He mentioned about the arthritic condition of the bones and that Alonzo ain't young."

We sat there by the fire for a long time while I tried to realize what all this meant. Neither one of us made a move to get to bed. After the fire died down I got up and put another stick on.

"What are we goin' to do, Auntie?"

Seemed like that question was the one she was waiting for to get her going again. She smiled at me, the same old Aunt Foster Mary smile that had warmed us all and kept us close and safe, no matter what kind of trouble was trying to get inside our house.

"Bud, you could be the richest and the healthiest man in Yakima County and you still wouldn't know when you got up in the morning what was going to lam you across the head before you got in bed that night. We're all sent our trials, the Meekins ain't got a corner on trouble, don't you ever think it. I always thanked the good Lord that so far He ain't never sent me one that I wasn't able to deal with, with His help." She reached over and patted me on the knee. "Ignorant and foolish woman that I am, I never realized until right now that He ain't ever goin' to, either." She rose from her chair and went over to put some water in the cocoa pans. Good night, I thought, I could at least have washed the dishes for her. I'm a fine helper, I am.

She poured a little soap in and said, "Let's let these soak until morning. Get to bed, hon. You've had a big day." She fixed the blankets on the old sofa for Amiella and went in to get her. I sat there and thought about what she had said and it wasn't until she'd tucked my little sister in and reached up to turn off the light that I thought, *She's* the one who's had a big day. I ain't done nothing but be in the wrong place at the wrong time. I could at *least* have carried Amiella out.

She pushed me gently toward the door to the lean-to and said, whispering, so she wouldn't wake up the kids, "We don't have to figure out all the answers at once, you know. Stop worryin'. We'll do the thing we have to do tomorrow and let day after tomorrow wait until day after tomorrow comes."

I nodded. I know I worry too much. She went on, "Just before Alonzo went to sleep he said, 'Well, Mary, it ain't as if you hadn't got a man in the house. Bud, he'll take care of you. If I'd listened to him I wouldn't be in this fix. He told me not to get up on that ladder alone. Sometimes I think that kid's got more sense than all the rest of us put together.'"

Seemed like I had just got to sleep when it was morning again. I heard a noise and, opening one eye, saw Lonnie reach down from the top bunk and tickle Bennie on his nose with a chicken feather. Bennie sneezed and woke up.

I opened my other eye and warned them, "Aunt Foster Mary didn't get home until 'way late last night. If you wake her up I'll lambaste you good. If you're hungry, I'll make your breakfast."

I got up and pulled on my pants and opened the door from the lean-to careful, so it wouldn't squeak.

"Don't be so quiet," Aunt Foster Mary said. "I want them all to wake up. I was going to call you as soon as I got Amiella's shoes polished. We're goin' to church."

"Walkin' will be too hard today, Auntie, there ain't no church close enough for us to get to. You and Amiella would never make it."

"You are goin' to drive us. Alonzo says you can drive our car just fine. He says you've driven it lots of times for him around the place here, and we're only going down near the school."

"Oh, O.K., fine." I was pleased, then I thought of something. "I thought you said Alonzo was going into surgery this morning?"

She was quiet a minute, her hands stopped over the little brown shoes. "He is, at ten o'clock. Best place for us to be, while he's in that operatin' room, is in church." She started shining again, and then went on, "Doctor says we won't do him no good there, waitin' and worryin'. He says Alonzo will be asleep for quite a while after."

"How you goin' to get in to the hospital, then?"

"I been thinkin' about what you said about Liz and Esther Holbrook still bein' here. Remember how she drove way over to see us a year ago last Labor Day? We were workin' at Millhouser's and they were down in the

113

lower valley, at that place. I bet she'd do it. Mr. Millhouser said to call him if I needed a ride, too, but I got to see Esther about somethin' else. I got a pot roast on. We could all come back here afterward."

So everybody got dressed fast and had breakfast.

"I need something warm," Auntie said. She put Mrs. Ransome's coat on and we started off. It had snowed enough last night so that it wasn't easy going, but Mr. Millhouser's snowplow had cleaned up the middle of the road real good and, boy, I stayed in the middle, the whole way. If another car had come along I might have had trouble, but I knew we wouldn't meet anybody on our road. After we got on the county road we went along real fast. Too fast, I guess. I was having fun driving and the little kids were really impressed at me taking Alonzo's place like that. We went by the family of a kid I know at school, Ward Farris, and his mouth hung open when we passed their big station wagon and he saw I was driving.

"Slow down, Bud, we got plenty of time," my aunt said. So I did. In fact, when we got to the church, we found out that the service didn't begin until ten o'clock and it wasn't quite nine thirty.

"Oh, well, we can drive around a little," I said, hoping we'd meet some more of the kids.

"We might as well look up the Holbrooks now, it ain't too early. Then if she can't drive me in, I can call Mr. Millhouser and let him know in plenty of time."

But the Holbrooks were home and awful glad to see us. They asked us in and apologized for the place.

"It's all I could get," Mrs. Holbrook told us. "I'm buyin' a typewriter for me and just paid for a new winter coat for

Liz. Now I'm goin' to find a better place. We hope we'll be in a nice room by Christmas."

"We already had Christmas!" cried Bennie and Lonnie.

"Good thing, too. If we hadn't," said my aunt, "we'd be havin' it without Alonzo." So then we told them about the accident and my aunt asked if Mrs. Holbrook could drive her in to Yakima Memorial to see Alonzo.

"Of course I will," she answered. "Be glad to. I remember how Alonzo helped us that time my husband took sick. Always hoped I could pay you back some day."

Then my aunt asked if she and Liz could come with us afterward for supper and they said yes, that would be fun. They finally decided that it might be a good idea to take the kids all home to our place after church.

"They can't see Alonzo, anyway, and they'd get too tired waitin'," Auntie said.

"I want to see Uncle Alonzo! How come I can't go?" Lonnie begged. "Please let me, Aunt Foster Mary!"

"No, love, they won't let little kids in. Write him a letter, why don't you? Draw him a nice picture. He'll likely be home tomorrow, I'd think."

Mrs. Holbrook was smiling at Lonnie. "You got another little nephew staying with you? What's this little boy's name?" she asked.

Lonnie hung his head and Bennie said, "His name's Lonnie." After a minute he added, "He's my brother." Mrs. Holbrook looked at them, Bennie stocky and brown-haired, and Lonnie so dark and thin, and she blinked her eyes but she didn't say anything. We got up to go to church.

Liz asked, "Would you care if I went too?" We said we

would like that and asked Mrs. Holbrook if she wouldn't like to go. She said, "I will next time, but I got to get the washing done if I'm going to be gone all day. You know how it is when you're working." She added, to my aunt, "I haven't got anything fit to wear, either. I haven't any winter clothes at all. Good thing I can wear blue jeans to work in the packing house."

She admired Mrs. Ransome's coat and Aunt Foster Mary said, "Ain't it lovely material? I'm making it into a coat for Amiella but I thought I'd wear it today. Don't quite meet here in front, though. The lady who owned it is a bit smaller than what I am." She laughed and Mrs. Holbrook did too.

"I'm so glad we found you home," Auntie said. "We'll be back sometime after eleven."

I watched Liz button up her new coat and I said, "Gee, you look nice, Liz!" and she said, "Thank you," and smoothed the blue fuzzy cloth down with her mittens.

"I like your hair that way, too," I told her and she tied a scarf under her chin and said, "I just washed it. It isn't quite dry yet, but I want to go with you. Miss McCarthy will be our Sunday School teacher, I think. I went once this year, but I thought church was at eleven so I was an hour late. It was almost over when I got there. She said to come again and I wanted to, but hated to go alone."

On the way there she said, "I like her, Miss McCarthy, don't you? All the kids do. She's pretty and she always listens to you like what you are saying is important."

"Yeah. She's really nice," I answered, "only I'm so dumb at this English stuff. I can't get heads nor tails out of it. For a long time now I been wanting to ask you how come you knew so much."

"Oh, I don't," Liz said. "I missed a lot of school, you know, moving and all, but it will be better now. For you, too."

"Boy, I hope so. Only one way to go when you are as dumb as I am; that's up, I guess. Will you help me sometimes? I think if I knew what she wants us to do, maybe I could do it. Usually I have even forgotten the directions by the time I get sat down to do the work."

"Sure. Any time."

We all filed into the church and took a seat near the back. The first thing was some hymns and prayers and then the minister gave a little talk intended especially for the children. Then he said that while the congregation was singing the next hymn the children would leave and go to their classes, so we did. Liz and I saw some kids about our age so we went in a little room after them and sure enough, there was Miss McCarthy. She didn't have school clothes on—she wore a red suit. She looked Christmasy. She had a pin on her jacket, too, a little green tree, all sparkly. Liz was right—she sure was pretty.

"I'm so glad you came, Wallace and Elizabeth," she told us. "The little ones are practicing for their part of the Christmas entertainment. Do you want to take them into the big Sunday School room down the hall?" Amiella was hanging onto my arm for dear life. Bennie and Lonnie dragged their feet about leaving me, too.

"It's their first time," I apologized. "Would it be all right if they stayed with me a little while until they get used to being here? They won't make any noise."

"Why don't you keep them today? We aren't having regular classes on account of the rehearsal, anyway. Last week my pupils offered to help any way they could but they thought the parts were intended more for younger children, so today I brought a Christmas story to read to those who aren't doing jobs elsewhere."

She got some smaller chairs for Amiella and the boys and then she opened a book. "This is a story by Leo Tolstoi. It's about a Russian cobbler named Adyevich who knew the people who walked down his street only by the shoes they wore, because he was very poor and his room was in the basement of an old building. All he could see were the feet of those who passed but he came to recognize many, even though they seldom came down his stairway."

Amiella and Bennie love stories. Lonnie was looking at Miss McCarthy and all the big kids but he started to listen too.

The teacher told how the old man's wife had died and his child, too, so he was all alone. When she came to the part about how sometimes at night he took out his wife's old shawl and the little red shoes, not even finished, that he had been making for his little boy when he got sick, Amiella just sat there, the tears running down her cheeks. I passed her a paper hankie to use and she did.

The teacher told about how Adyevich read his Bible at night and that he said he wished that he had lived in those times because he would have liked to listen to Jesus and talk to him, too. See, the old man was so lonesome he used to talk out loud to himself, on account of hardly ever seeing anybody else.

Miss McCarthy went on, her voice sounding like the music of a waterfall I heard once when we stopped the car along the road, down in Oregon. She told how he put the shoes back in the chest where he kept them with the Bible, and folded the old shawl and all of a sudden that word "shawl" got me. I thought about Aunt Foster Mary putting hers over her shoulders to come out in the cold to meet us and then I had another picture of Alonzo folding that shawl and putting it away and I thought to myself, "I got to get out of here! I'm going to cry myself!"

I thought about going for a drink of water, but just then I caught sight of Liz and she had such a sad look on her face that I decided maybe everybody felt the same. No disgrace, I guess.

Miss McCarthy was a real storyteller, I thought, listening to the rest. I had missed part of it about some people had been to see him, all right, the particular day this story was about, and I heard her stop and say, "Isn't it a good thing that Amiella stayed?" She looked at one of the older girls. "If we decided to dramatize this story, Carol, you could be the soldier's wife and Amiella could be her little girl, the one who gets the red shoes. Let's try that part, shall we?"

Amiella was already on her feet, her hand in the big girl's. All it took was the word "shoes"—she was standing there, her mouth kind of open and her eyes shining like stars.

Then Miss McCarthy said, "I know we only have one more Sunday before Christmas but we could do this partly in pantomime. I could read the story and you could act it out. Let's try it, shall we?"

So she read again about Adyevich calling the soldier's

wife and the little girl and telling them to come in and get warm because they were walking a long way to join the father, and they were cold and shivering. He didn't have much to eat, Adyevich, but he shared his black bread with them and he made some tea. Before they left, he opened his chest and got out the shoes and after he had finished them, he gave them to the little girl.

Miss McCarthy motioned to me and before I knew it, I was over there next to her and Amiella was sticking her foot out and I was pretending to put a shoe on it. Then she borrowed Liz's scarf and gave it to me and I laid it over Carol's shoulders.

"That was fine," she said, quietly, with a special smile for Amiella. "Now the next scene is where the little boy steals the apple from the woman on the corner and she leaves her fruit stand and chases him and he runs down Adyevich's steps. Why don't we have *two* little boys? First . . ." she put her hand on his shoulder and I said, "Bennie." Then she said, "And then, when the apple woman starts running . . ." "Lonnie," I told her, and she went on, "Lonnie steals an apple, too, and they run around and around the square."

We did that part. Those kids really entered in. Liz was the apple woman and she enjoyed it too. Everybody laughed when she almost caught them and they got away and ran down the steps.

"Stop them, Adyevich. Talk to them," Miss McCarthy said, and just like I always do, scolding those kids and yet sticking up for them, too, I said, grabbing Liz and holding her, "Wait a minute. They didn't mean any harm!" I looked at Lonnie's thin little face and remembered him

120

under that bed, crying, the first day I ever saw him. Forgetting the real words, I said to Liz, "Haven't *you* ever been hungry?"

She was great. She said, "But I'm poor, too! They stole my apples!"

"I'll pay for them," I answered, "O.K.? Say, why don't all of you stay and have a little tea? And—er—some of this here black bread. I got a little left." So everybody sat down and pretended to eat.

"You were absolutely wonderful, all of you!" Miss McCarthy cried, and just then a bell rang. "Oh, dear, church is over. Wallace, take my book home and read the part. Practice it at home, will you? Let's not have a pantomime, after all. You have a lovely deep voice, Wallace, and Adyevich's part should never be read by a woman. We can practice again next Sunday and be ready to give it on Christmas Eve."

"I can't!" I said, and I nearly died when my voice came out a high squeak. I got it back down again and tried over. This time I made it real deep. "I can't, Miss McCarthy, I've never been in a play before in my life!"

"Of course you can," she answered. "You're a natural. You practice now. But don't worry about learning it word for word. Just think of the meaning like you did today. I have to hurry and catch the minister. I'll ask him to do the Voice from offstage in the last scene. Good-bye, now."

"We're going to be in a Christmas play!" the kids yelled as soon as they saw Aunt Foster Mary, and the people around her smiled. One lady shook hands with Auntie and said, "Do come next Sunday! Merry Christmas!" And Aunt Foster Mary smiled, too, and said "Merry Christmas!" We shook hands with the minister, Mr. Wilson, and he said, too, to be sure to come back and we said we would.

"Nice to belong some place, ain't it?" my aunt said to Liz and Liz said yes, she sure hoped they could stay: she and her mother liked the Yakima country best of any place they had ever lived.

"I even like winter," Liz smiled, "now I got a coat to wear."

Her mother was ready for the trip. "I'll have to wear these, it's all I've got," she said, looking down at her jeans as she pulled on a jacket. "But I guess nobody I know will see me anyway."

"You look fine," my aunt told her. When we got home she took care of the fire, looked at the meat and said, "Bud, put the potatoes in at five o'clock. But if we ain't home by the time they are getting soft, pull the frying pan way back on the stove." Then she put away Mrs. Ransome's nice coat and got out her old one.

We told them we'd watch the dinner and the kids. Then Lonnie and Ben and Amiella each made a picture for Alonzo, and Auntie and Mrs. Holbrook went off to the hospital.

We ate some of the Christmas candy and we practiced the play a while. Then Liz showed us how to play a game. We got an old deck of cards and I said, "I don't even think they're all here. You know, the kids have been playing with them."

She said it didn't matter, and told me to turn them all face down all over the table.

"I want to play! Can we play, too?" asked Lonnie. She said sure, all of us could play.

"Now, Lonnie, you be first. Turn over one card. Leave it where it is and turn over another. Look! They're both kings! You get to keep them because they match!" Lonnie was so excited he didn't know what to do. The next time he got a six and a ten. "Well, you got one pair. Now, give Amiella a turn. When you miss you have to wait until we get all the way around again."

We played until all the cards were gone. Bennie won. He had two more pairs than anybody else.

"He really concentrated. That's the name of this game: Concentration," Liz told them. "Now you know how. You three play another one by yourselves. We'll be back."

We checked the fire and the meat. It wasn't time to put in the potatoes yet. I wondered how Alonzo was, wondered when Auntie would get back.

Liz and I sat down on the old sofa and talked about being on the road and campfires at night and what we liked best about California: that was all the sunshine and getting to go in swimming sometimes, of course; and what we liked about Medford and that was that California was too hot by that time and Oregon was a nice change, and awful green and pretty, too. Then I said, "Yakima?" and she said, "Yakima got to be like home. We couldn't wait to get back. Ma and I both want to stay."

I said, "We do, too. My Aunt Foster Mary says she wants to look outside every day for the rest of her life and see that valley. But I don't know. I don't know where we'll go now." I told her all about the work Alonzo had promised to do and now he couldn't.

"But your uncle can't help it that he had a bad accident! Mr. Ransome wouldn't kick him out for that, would he?"

"Alonzo wouldn't be able to earn the money," I pointed

out. "Uncle might be laid up a long time according to Aunt Foster Mary and how could he do the work?"

"Think of something. I sure hope you get to stay." She looked around. "You got such a nice house. It's pretty, isn't it?"

It did look awful pretty with the little tree and the new floor. I began to get an idea when I looked at the floor, but I thought I'd better think about it some more, so I changed the subject, and asked her again how it was that she savvied all that English stuff.

"I like to read," she said. "I was sick almost all the first year of school. I had rheumatic fever and I was in the hospital for a long time. When I could sit up and felt a little better, a lady used to come to catch me up on my school work. My Ma was working and couldn't come in the daytime so I was really glad to see that teacher. I was so lonesome. She was the only visitor I had, except when my Mom could come. She was nice to me and reading was fun. I remember she told me to learn to know books and I would never be lonesome. And she was right. They are a heck of a lot better than most of the people I've known." After a while she went on. "When I went home from the hospital, I still couldn't go back to school for months and another lady, a home teacher they called her, came and taught me. Not every day, but two or three times a week. I liked her, too. Anyway, I got to be a pretty good reader, and most things are easy if you like to read. I want to go to Yakima Junior College."

She wasn't kidding. She meant it.

"You do? What for?" I asked her and she said, "So I'll *be* somebody, that's what for. And it doesn't cost too much. My Ma is brushing up on her typing so she can maybe get an office job in Yakima someday. She's going to Junior College nights, next quarter, if we can get a secondhand car, and she's going to save all she can and I'm going to work in the fruit every year and save all I can and somehow I'm going to college. But I got to get good grades, so that's why I study."

"My aunt is set on us going, too, but I don't know about that."

"Sure, you ought to. Take a look at all the people we know who didn't go to school. See how old they look by the time they are thirty-five. See what happens to you when you have to work like that all your life and never have a decent place to live in or any decent furniture or clothes. And then later you look at what it's doing to your kids, and by that time it's already too late for you. Most pickers give up. They die young, too, because of the kind of life they have to live."

I thought when I heard her say all that, it might be what Aunt Foster Mary had been thinking for years but not saying because it would hurt Alonzo.

I guess those kids played eight or nine games of Concentration. They were crazy about it. And do you know what, Bennie won every single time. He never forgot where a card was, once it had been turned over.

"Bennie," I told him, "I think we are going to have to send you to college. You are a pretty sharp little guy."

Liz grinned. Lonnie said, "I almost beat him last time! I knew where those last pairs were, too, but it was his turn first."

"That settles it. We'll send you, too."

Amiella came up and held on to my hand. "You want to go too, Little Bug?" I asked her.

She was thinking about something else. "Bud, do I get to keep them? Oh, I hope they are for me!"

"What, hon?"

"Those little red shoes that you are going to give me in the Christmas play."

13 "Esther, I was so glad when Bud told me you were still here. Old friends are best—'specially when you are having troubles. Thanks ever so much for driving me in to see Alonzo," Auntie said. "We'll see you again real soon, won't we?"

"I should say so. Christmas Eve, anyway. We'll have to go to see that play. But, Mary, just let me know if you need me to drive you—anytime. Or to help out with the kids. Good night, kids. Good night, Bud."

"Thanks again ever so much for driving me to the hospital," my aunt said. "We didn't get much chance to talk, but we will next time."

"You're welcome. Thank *you* for the good dinner."

Liz said, "I had fun, too, Bud. I sure hope your uncle gets better soon."

They went into their motel room and we all drove home. It would have been a nice day if only Alonzo had been with us.

Aunt Foster Mary, like always, was reading my mind.

"He's in a lot of pain, his leg aches from the bone right out, but in the hospital they can give him something when the pain gets too bad. The doctor says he has to stay at least a week."

"I thought he could come home tomorrow, maybe!"

"No, they want to keep him where they can watch out for him—try to keep infection from starting. And in a week they are going to take more X rays to see that the pin is in place."

"Oh."

"He won't be able to do any physical work until spring."

What will we do? I thought, and she answered that, too.

"I talked to Esther about working in the packing house and she thinks I can get in. I'll wait until Alonzo is back with us. He and Amiella will have to take care of each other when she gets home from kindergarten. I been thinkin' of some things to do to keep him busy and make the time go by faster. It ain't going to be easy, though. There's never been a time when he ain't had two or three projects ahead of him."

"Well, we'll have to think of some he can do sitting still," I said, "like fixing all that furniture. I think I can make him a little workbench that he can wheel his chair under, for hammering and sawing. Then, maybe I ought to make one a little lower so that he can sand things and paint them. I'll fix it so the legs will be on casters and he can move it easy."

But we both knew Alonzo would find it hard to get used to that kind of life. What I was worrying about most was whether we could stay where we were. Again she went right on answering what I hadn't got around to asking yet.

She lowered her voice. The kids in the back seat were almost asleep. "Do you think we need to tell Mr. Ransome before he gets back from California? I was thinking there must be some way we can do part of the work, to pay for staying there. And, after all, Alonzo did what the boss told him to do. He fixed up the cottage first, and he done a good job, too."

"Yeah. Well, all depends, I guess, on whether he writes Alonzo and tells him to do some kind of work that we can't do for him."

"Or have somebody else do." My aunt had been going back and forth over this whole business, squirreling a little hope here and a little luck there, just like I had before I went to sleep. But I had to step on this one. She had forgotten one important thing.

"Auntie, we don't have much money. And we owe. We got a couple of bills in town and Alonzo's accident is going to cost a heap of money." She thought a while and I went on, "I was thinking about that, maybe hiring somebody from around here to do some of the jobs: like putting in the shower and toilet cabin for the pickers. I think Alonzo was strong for that and he hoped to win Mr. Ransome over by saying he could do the installation himself. But we ain't got the money to have somebody else do it."

"Mr. Millhouser told me to quit worryin' about the hospital and doctor bills. He says he carries insurance on his workers and he's sure Mr. Ransome does, too."

Well, if that was so, it helped a heap. But maybe we had to pay part. I knew it cost a lot to stay in the hospital a whole week. And Alonzo might be there even longer.

We turned the corner and drove up to the little cottage. I stopped the car and neither one of us made a move to get out. That big old moon was right behind the chimney of our house and the snow on the roof kind of sparkled like the shiny stuff they put on Christmas cards. I was afraid to look at Aunt Foster Mary. I didn't know as I ought to come any closer to what she was thinking. It ain't possible, I guess, for a man to know how some women feel about the place they settle down in and keep clean and try to make pretty so that their family will be glad to come back to it, no matter where else they go. All I knew was that my aunt had waited a long time to get hers and if there was anything I could do to help her keep it for a little while, I was sure going to do it. I had to admit right now, though, that things looked discouraging.

Finally I turned to Auntie. Her face was calm and peaceful; she had made up her mind. For the first time since Alonzo's accident, the worry lines had disappeared. We got out and she opened the rear door and reached for Amiella.

"Open the door for us," I whispered. "I'll bring her. Wake up, boys. You are going to have to walk. I can't carry all three of you." But I could, I thought, I could if I had to. I could carry all the things Alonzo had been carrying, because somebody had to and he wasn't here now.

We put Amiella down on the sofa and the boys stumbled off to bed in the lean-to. Auntie reached up to turn off the light and then in the darkness of the little room she put her wet cheek up against mine. When I felt the tears, I put my arm around her and I was surprised to hear a little soft laugh.

"Well, love," she said, "tonight we had a big hassle over all the things we can't do. Tomorrow let's get up early and make a good start on the ones we can."

14   "I thought we were going to have a vacation this week," Lonnie said the next morning. "I want to go sleddin'."

"That's tough," I told him. "The roads are fine now. False alarm. Your days off will begin a week from tomorrow, Christmas vacation, unless we have another big snow."

"Auntie," I called to her from the lean-to, "I'm taking the pickup. I have to go in and have a little talk with Alonzo, O.K.? I really need to see him. I'll be careful."

"No, Bud. I know you can drive. I just don't want you to get in any trouble. Mrs. Millhouser will take you in after school. You go instead of me. Alonzo will be tickled to death. He misses you kids an awful lot."

"Auntie, I can't just go and ask Mrs. Millhouser to drive me eighteen miles in to Yakima."

"You don't have to. I forgot to tell you she came over here while we were in church to see if she could do anything to help. When she didn't find us home, she and Mr. Millhouser drove in to town and stopped by to see Alonzo, but he wasn't awake yet, from the anesthetic. They were just leavin' when we got there. She explained to me that her mother is in a nursing home in Yakima and hasn't been very well, so they try to get in every day or so to see her anyway. They both said we wouldn't be puttin' them out a mite to take us along when they went."

"Well, all right. I'll get off the school bus at their place and see what she says. So if I don't come home when the kids do, you'll know where I am, O.K.?"

To Lonnie I said, "We never did get that sled down for you. So you can't go sledding anyhow. But don't worry, I'll do it as soon as I have somebody along to help me. Maybe Mr. Millhouser will stop by a minute tonight. This snow will be with us for a while, boy. Don't fret about *that*."

When we got ready to go, Auntie said, "I think it would be all right for you to take the car as far as the main road. You could leave it there until you get back."

I knew it would, but I didn't need to drive the car really, so I shook my head. She thought I needed the car to feel grown-up, or something, but I figured she had enough to worry about already. "We can walk, it ain't bad at all. I been out in front and there's no new snow. We got to get going, though, or we'll miss the bus."

So we slogged on out to the county road. It was fun in the morning, when you weren't tired and you were full of a good, warm breakfast. The air was clear and cold but there wasn't any wind today and we made it in no time. Amiella was coming later with the mother of one of the kindergarten kids, but the car would be full so there wouldn't be room for us anyway.

Emily Millhouser smiled and waved before I even got to the corner where the bus stops. I went over where she was standing to talk to her. I looked around after a few minutes and Bennie was with two little boys, not talking, just grinning at them. Lonnie was behind him, scowling at all the kids who were horsing around, laughing and throwing snow at each other. Nobody had better take a chance and throw snow on him, I thought, or there will be fireworks, and just then somebody did. A big girl with a red coat and a scarf over her head tossed a soft piece of snow and it landed on his shoulders. He balled up his fists and she said, "Hi, Lonnie! Where's Amiella?"

It was Carol. She smiled at him and after a minute or so, he smiled back and said, "She gets picked up now." He looked at her uncertainly for a minute to be sure the smile was there, I guess, and then decided she was his friend. He reached down and grabbed a hunk of snow and threw it as hard as he could at her. She ducked and instead of getting it in the middle, she caught it on her face. "You fiend!" she cried and took off after him. He ran like everything and she pretended not to be able to catch him. They were both winded and laughing when the bus came. She scrambled on first and got a good seat near the front. When Ed Hanson tried to sit by her, she said, "Sorry, this seat's taken." Lonnie came down the aisle looking for me

134

but I was sitting with Emily. Then he looked for Bennie and he was in between the two little boys. He started for the back of the bus and Carol reached out and pulled his jacket. He stopped scowling, grinned at her and sat down. I don't know what they were talking about. I couldn't hear after the bus started up, but his tongue was going a mile a minute and he was showing off like everything. She laughed at anything he said.

When we got to school, I leaned down and whispered to him, "I thought you didn't like girls."

He looked at me with surprise. "That was Carol," he said. "She's in the play, don't you remember?"

That night I told Bennie and Lonnie that I was going to Millhouser's and they were to hustle on home.

Mrs. Millhouser said as soon as she saw me at her door, "Oh, you are going in today! I bet your uncle will be glad to see you. Wait just a minute, Bud, and I'll get my coat and the car keys."

Mrs. Millhouser is nice and friendly-looking. Emily looks a lot like her.

When she came back, she was carrying a little radio. "Do you think Alonzo would like this? It belongs to my oldest boy, but we've got two others here in the house—he doesn't need it. Alonzo looked so lonesome when we came in his room the other day. It must get tiresome just lying there, in pain, and with nothing to do. Maybe this will cheer him a bit."

"Gee," I said, "he would really like it. That is sure nice of you."

I held it on my lap on the way in. When we got there, she said, "I'm not coming in yet, Bud. I'll go and see my mother first and stop to say hello to Alonzo on the way back. And then I have a little shopping to do, so if there is anything you need, you'll have a chance to get it."

I thanked her and she drove off. I went inside and asked a lady at the desk how I could find Alonzo Meekin and she told me the room number after she looked on some cards. I went up in the elevator. There was a strong kind of medicine smell in the halls. In every room some man was lying there in the bed, the ones with visitors smiling and talking, and the ones who were alone, sad-looking and quiet. Some of them had their eyes closed. In one big room I saw an old fellow way over by the window who looked like he was dead and I thought, Well, we got something to be thankful for and that's that Alonzo only broke his leg. He could easy have broken his neck. I looked again at the number on the door. It was Alonzo's room and the old man by the window was Alonzo.

I tiptoed over past two other sleeping men and he heard me and opened his eyes. At first he didn't seem to know me and then his eyes lit up. "How are you, Son?" he asked. "It sure is good to see you."

"Good to see you, Uncle. How you feeling?"

"Not up to climbin' any ladders for a while, but I'm doing O.K."

"Look, Alonzo. Look what Mrs. Millhouser sent you to use while you're here in the hospital." I leaned down and plugged in the little radio and fixed it on his bedside table. The other men sat up and watched and Alonzo said, "Meet my son. Bud, this is Mr. Watson and Mr. O'Connor." One was a real old fellow, thin and feeble. Mr. O'Connor was about Alonzo's age and looked like he'd be real good company.

Alonzo patted the radio. "Now ain't that fine! I will enjoy hearin' the news and everything. Often wished I had one of these." He was really touched, I could tell.

I reached in my pocket and said, "I brought you something, too. Somehow your good old knife got left on the shed floor where Auntie used it when she was binding up your leg. I figured you'd be lost without this."

He reached out and took it and his eyes twinkled. "You don't just happen to have a little old piece of wood on you, do you?"

"Happens I do," I answered and brought out a couple of small blocks I had picked up from the lumber shed.

"I could make a doll for Amiella. Ask your aunt to bring along a strong rubber band or a piece of elastic from her sewing box next time she comes, will you? Them dolls we got at the dime store don't even move their legs. I could make a better doll than that with both hands tied behind me."

He fiddled with the radio a few minutes but turned it off and said, "I'd rather talk to you. This will sure be nice to have when I'm alone, though."

"Alonzo, how much were you figurin' on payin' for a shower stall for that cabin?"

"The man in the hardware store had some others comin' in, he said, that might not be as high as the one he showed me that night we bought all the stuff. I thought I'd wait and see, and then check Sears' catalog and get whichever one was the cheapest. But no use askin' about it now. By the time I was able to install a shower and all that, my job would be long gone. We'll let somebody else worry about prices."

"I was just askin'. Alonzo, that roofing stuff comes in one sheet but it ain't wide enough to cover the whole roof. How were you figurin' on doin' that?"

"You cut a piece just big enough to cover the one side, see? Then another the same size for the other side. Then you cut a strip about twenty inches wide and you put it just over the ridgepole, about ten inches on each side, see what I mean?" He took a pencil and showed me on the back of an envelope. "Least, I've done that before, and it worked out all right; the overlapping piece sheds the rain and it can't get through on top, see?"

"I get it. I was just wonderin'. I happened to see that stuff and I thought about it the other day."

All of a sudden a look of alarm came on his face. "Boy, if you try to get up on that roof in this kind of weather, you'll break your fool neck! If I even hear you mentioning it, I'll break it for you! Promise me, now, that you won't think up nothing crazy while I'm in the hospital."

I laughed. "It's a cinch I won't do it this week, Alonzo, and you'll be home soon, so you can supervise any jobs I try to do. I promise."

He looked relieved, then grinned kind of sheepishly and said, "No, Bud, you wouldn't be the one to climb a ladder alone with ice on the roof. I'm a fine one to be telling you to be careful. It's just that I ain't got nothing to do but to lay here worryin'."

"Well, don't worry about us. We will take good care of the kids, Auntie and me."

"And, Bud, take good care of her, won't you? Don't let her work too hard and get sick. And take care of yourself."

I told him sure and we talked some more about fixing

up the cabins and what all Mr. Ransome had told him to do to them. I just acted like I was sort of interested in it and he smiled when he answered me and I knew he thought I was only tryin' to get his mind off his troubles and his pain.

He began to look pretty tired and I said, "Let's turn on the radio. I guess it ain't time for the news but here's some nice music. Shut your eyes, Alonzo, and rest a bit."

He went to sleep and I sat there and watched him. No wonder Auntie had come home looking so worried after she saw him yesterday. He was thin and white, an old man. He didn't look like he'd ever work again. All of a sudden I knew that was what he was afraid of—that he'd never be able to take care of us. Maybe he was even afraid he couldn't ever walk again.

Mrs. Millhouser came and he woke up and thanked her for the radio. She could tell he was awful pleased about that. Before we left, he said, "Give the baby a big hug for me. I miss her like everything. And tell them two rapscallions to behave, and mind you and their auntie, or I'll skin them alive when I get home." His voice was so thin and quavery I could hardly hear what he said.

"Sure, Alonzo. And you eat a lot and take your medicine and get strong, hear me?"

"Yeah, I will. Bud?"

"Yes, Uncle?"

"Next time you come, see if you can bring me a bigger chunk of wood. Maybe a little walnut or mahogany. Think you could find some someplace?"

"You bet." I patted him on the shoulder and he reached up and grabbed my hand. I went down the hall with a great big lump in my throat. Mrs. Millhouser seemed to understand and she didn't talk until we got to the stores.

"I'm going to be about half an hour, Bud. You can come with me or meet me here."

"Can I help you in any way?"

"No, no heavy packages, just some odds and ends still to pick up for Mother for Christmas."

"Then if it's all right with you, I'll meet you here."

I checked the hardware store and they had the new shower stalls. I wrote down the price and hurried to Sears. They had some a couple of dollars cheaper, so I ordered one and said I would pick it up Saturday. I thought to myself, if this doesn't work out, if Auntie says no, I'll call them and cancel the order. I looked at the toilets and washbasins and picked out the least expensive, and said to include that. I wrote down all the prices carefully and added them up, so I could tell Auntie.

Mrs. Millhouser wasn't at the car yet so I looked in my pocket and found a little change. I went in a grocery store and bought an all-day sucker for each of the kids and a candy bar for Aunt Foster Mary.

I really felt like I was Alonzo when the kids for the first time went through my pockets as soon as I got home. They found the candy and I said, just like Uncle, "Well, now, how'd that get there? I felt it but I thought it was a piece of chewin' tobacca."

Everybody waited, grinning, while I searched all through every pocket, shaking my head and finally handing the candy bar to Auntie and saying, "Here's a chew for you, too, Mary." The little boys laughed and laughed. Aunt Foster Mary smiled and said, like she always did, "All you kids put your candy here in the cupboard until after supper."

They had waited for me and everybody was hungry, so I washed my hands and sat down. I picked up my knife, thinking it sure was strange for Alonzo to be missing, and planning some things I wanted to talk to Aunt about when the little kids were in bed. There was a big silence all around the table. I looked at them. Every head was bowed. They were waiting for me to be Uncle again.

Finally I put down my knife and said, "Dear Lord, we thank You for this food and for our children. Make Alonzo well fast. And whatever it is You got in mind for us to do, Lord, show us how to do it. And forgive us for our mistakes. Amen."

15 Every night after school that whole week I met Liz in Miss McCarthy's room and we went over the lines I had to say in the play. Miss McCarthy said, "Don't worry so much, Wallace. The only time you have to make a long speech is in the last scene and the Bible is right there on your knee. If you forget what to say, put this paper here, look down at the Bible, and read it off." But I learned all the lines by heart anyway. I didn't want Auntie to be ashamed of me and I was hoping Alonzo would be home by then, too. He'd get a big kick out of the little kids being in a Christmas play. We all wanted to do it right. The kids could hardly wait until Christmas Eve.

We only got to practice a few minutes because we had to take the bus. As soon as I got home I would change to my old clothes and hurry over to the second cabin. Aunt Foster Mary had swept it out and scrubbed the walls. She'd have the fire going in the old stove and would be busy painting, with Amiella drawing pictures at the table. While Auntie painted, I put the little linoleum squares in place. We had decided that we were going to have one cabin all done, if we could, by the time Alonzo got home from the hospital. We knew that would cheer him up more than anything could.

After supper, if Auntie went in town with the Millhousers or with Mrs. Holbrook to see Alonzo, I'd bring the kids over to play in the cabin. They'd have a few games of Concentration and I'd do some more work on the floor. Friday she let me take the pickup to school and wait until Mrs. Holbrook got through work. While we were waiting for her to come home, we all practiced the play, even the little kids.

"You sound exactly like Miss McCarthy, Liz," Lonnie said, while she was reading it out loud to us.

"It's just because you are used to hearing her read these same words," Liz said.

"No," I told her, surprised that Lonnie had noticed this, too. "It's something about your voice. It's so soft, like music. I really like to hear you."

"Well, if my voice sounds like hers, it's the only way I am like Miss McCarthy," she answered, her face all pink. "Now, if I looked like her, I wouldn't care if I had a voice like a foghorn."

"What's a voice like a foghorn, Liz?" Amiella asked. So

she tooted way down low like a little old boat far out in the water and we all laughed.

Mrs. Holbrook came home and drove us out to the orchards and then, after we ate supper together, she and Auntie went in to see Alonzo.

I took Liz over to show her the cabin. It really looked nice now. I knew Uncle would like it and Mr. Ransome, too. She thought we had done a real good job, but of course, she hadn't seen what a mess it was before we started.

"I've seen plenty others like it, though," she said. "All I have to say is, any picker would be tickled to death to live here. I wish I could. It's sure better than our old motel room."

We went back to the cottage and Amiella asked her to read a story. "My teacher read this one today," Sis said, handing her the book. "I asked her to read it all over again because I love cats, but she didn't have time to so she said I could take it home if I'd be very careful. It's a liberry book."

"What's the name of the book?" Liz asked and Amiella traced the three words with her finger and said, "Hundreds of Cats, Thousands of Cats, Millions and Billions and Trillions of Cats." Everybody laughed and Lonnie opened his mouth to correct her, but I kicked him and he shut up.

"Good for you," Liz said. "O.K., I'll read it, and you help me."

So she read the story about the lonely old man and old woman who decided that a cat was just what they needed. Even the little boys chimed in at the end when the little old man said they had found the most beautiful one: "And

I ought to know, because I've seen hundreds of cats, thousands of cats, millions and billions and trillions of cats!"

"I wish I had a cat," sighed Amiella. "In my whole, whole life I haven't never had a cat."

"Well, you never had a house before, hon," I told her. "First you get a house, then you get a cat. I expect you"ll get one some day."

"I sure hope it's before I'm a very old lady," she said, her mind still on the story. "Why do you suppose they waited so long to look for a cat?"

"Beats me," I said, "unless they were pickers. Time for bed, now. O.K., you guys. On the double!"

"How come we have to go to bed when we got company?" Lonnie asked.

"How come you only argue about going to bed when Aunt Foster Mary ain't here? Because Liz is my company, that's why. And we are going to study and we got to have a little peace to do it in."

After they left, I groaned and said, "How come I always say 'ain't'? I know better—the teachers have told me often enough. I guess I'll always talk like an apple picker."

"No, you won't. That part's easy."

"Yeah? Alonzo says 'ain't', Auntie says 'ain't', all the kids say 'ain't'. It's only at school I hear people talk a different way. How'm I ever going to learn?"

She thought about it for a minute and then wrote on a slip of paper. I read it when she got through. "I am not going. Lonnie isn't going, either. We aren't going to school today."

I laughed and said, "You better change this to Bennie.

Lonnie would be only too willing to believe it. O.K., I'll try this out every day."

Then we got our school books and worked on Language Arts. We had to write a paragraph called "What I Would Like to Do More Than Anything Else."

"I asked Miss McCarthy if she meant when we get through school or next summer or tonight or what and she said it will be much more interesting if we all think she meant something different," I told Liz and she said, "I think so, too."

We each took a piece of paper and she said, "Let's write down any ideas we have. Then in a few minutes we'll talk about them. Just write anything. Let's not worry about punctuation or spelling or anything like that. If I know Miss McCarthy, she thinks ideas are more important, anyway."

I wrote down "More Than Anything Else" and I knew those words were spelled right because Liz had copied down the assignment and I had copied it from her paper. I thought and thought and then I finished, ". . .I would like to one an orcherd and grow apples. I would have about fourty acers-or at lease 30. I would by my orcherd in the upper yakima vally and no place else because that is the best place in the whole world to grow apples." I passed it to her, "How many mistakes did I make?"

"Don't worry about that. I think you have a good paragraph. I'll correct the mistakes, if you want me to."

"O.K. And tell me why. Oh, yeah, I get it. No capitals because those words ain't"— I pounded my fist on the table—"*aren't* in the title, I knew that."

She went ahead and corrected what I had written, and I

forgot to watch the paper. I was watching how her soft hair fell over her face while she wrote. Same color as Amiella's, I thought, only instead of being wispy, it was all shiny and heavy. I never remembered her having such pretty hair before.

I tried to pay attention while she told me about the other mistakes. When she got through, I said, "Thanks a lot. I'll copy it over in a few minutes. Want some cocoa?"

"Fine." This time I tasted it first and added more sugar and I said, "I make pretty good cocoa if I do say it myself."

"Yes, you sure do."

Then I said, "O.K., now you read me yours." I sat down on the old sofa with my cup of cocoa and she brought hers over and sat down at the other end, her papers in her hand. She took a drink of her cocoa and smiled at me and then she read: "I want to do so many things I can't decide which one to write about. I want to get locked up in the Yakima County Library the night it starts to snow. I want the snow to get so deep that no one can get to the library, not even the librarian. I want that snowstorm to last until I have read all the books I haven't already read. Because I have never had a chance to read as long as I want to without being interrupted."

She took a deep breath and looked up, and then went on: "Down in California I saw a place where there was a sign that said, 'All the orange juice you can drink for ten cents.' I stood there a long time and watched the people go in and drink orange juice. If I ever go back there I have ten cents now and I am going in and I will probably stay all day." She peeked at me again and I said, "Wow! You

147

wrote a lot!" Then she finished: "What I really want more than anything is for my mother and me to get to stay here and not go on the road anymore. I want to have a little house with nice furniture and I want to have a pretty dress to wear just on Sunday and I want to go to college. When I finish college I want to be a librarian, I think, or maybe an actress, if I turn out to be pretty enough."

"I bet you will," I said and she said, "I'm going to cross that out, that last part. We might have to read them in class."

I started to say, "There's some more on the back of the page," but she put it under her book fast, so I didn't. I copied mine over carefully and when she went to get a drink of water I sneaked a look and it said, "What I really want, after I do all those other things, is to marry somebody nice and have four children, because an only child gets too lonesome. I don't want any of my children ever to be lonesome."

16 Aunt Foster Mary came home from the hospital two nights before Christmas Eve and said, "I saw the doctor and he doesn't think Alonzo can leave by Christmas, like I'd hoped. He asked if he could call us and when I said we didn't have no phone, Mrs. Millhouser spoke up and said, 'I'll see you get the message. And we'll go get you whenever the doctor says Alonzo can come home.' So I thanked her, and Dr. Lawrence said, 'Well, I'll let you know after we take the next X rays.'"

We were all pretty sad about this because we had figured on Alonzo maybe getting to see the kids in the Christmas program and besides, we missed him a lot. He had already been gone ten days. I knew Auntie wouldn't worry about him so much once she got him home again. He just wasn't eating at the hospital. He said the food was good, real good, but he didn't have any appetite, eating alone and in bed. It just didn't seem natural.

"Of course, he ain't getting any exercise, either," Aunt Foster Mary told me. "I think he could go up and down the hall in the wheelchair, but the nurses are so busy he don't like to bother them to help him get in it. He told me that if they let him wear his own clothes then he'd think he was really going somewhere, but he was dad-blamed if he was going to go parading down the halls with nothing much more'n a nightshirt on and all those visitors comin' and goin'."

I would be glad to see Alonzo because I could hardly wait to show him what we had been doing. Mr. Millhouser had taken his truck last Saturday when we went in town and we had brought back the stuff for the shower room. Aunt Mary had been at the painting, and it all looked bright and new. We had a new hot water tank, too. But we couldn't put in any pipes. The ground was like cement. We could do it later, when Alonzo could supervise. Alonzo would never believe it, so no use telling him until he came home. I told Liz the debt we owed our good neighbors, the Millhousers, was like the one we might owe the hospital—I tried to think of the right word and she said, "Astronomical," and I said yes, it sure was.

The night before Chirstmas Eve Auntie got Mrs. Holbrook to drive her to Millhouser's. She took one of her fruitcakes, two loaves of fresh-baked bread, and a ginger cake. She gave the same to Mrs. Holbrook.

"Right now, it's the only way I have of sayin' 'thank you' for all you've done," she told them. "Merry Christmas!"

I drove the car home but before we left the motel, Liz whispered to me, "I got a present for you, too, but you have to get it tomorrow night after the play. Don't tell the kids." I figured when she said "you" she meant all of us, and I wondered what it was.

Auntie let me drive the car to the church Christmas Eve. It was clear and cold out. It was early, not even four o'clock, but beginning to get dark and a few stars were shining, but no moon yet. The children we saw when we went inside were all dressed up. I thought ours didn't look too bad. The boys had their new stuff on and Auntie had made over a dress for Amiella and finished her new coat, and put her hair up on rags, so she thought she was really something special. I wished I could take a picture of her for Alonzo, the way her face looked when she saw the children's choir all decked out in their white dresses and silvery pie-tin halos. I thought of the special surprise for Amiella, and patted a bulge in my pocket.

We had to stay in a little room, the minister's study Miss McCarthy said it was, so we didn't get to see much of the first part of the program. People came through when their parts were over, and went out the other door so they could sit in the audience and watch the rest of the pageant. We heard the music real good, though, and when the door opened, Liz and I would peek out and see her mother and my aunt sitting in the very middle of the front row. They didn't want to miss a thing.

At the end of the last scene, the big floodlights were on

the manger and a great big star was shining up above the little stable. It was dark everywhere else, so we crowded to the door and looked out.

"Sh!" said Miss McCarthy, "get ready, now!"

My knees started knocking together and the palms of my hands got wet. The lights all went on for a minute and then every light in the whole place went out. There was some scurrying around and some pushing of buttons and finally we heard Mr. Wilson, the minister, say, calm and quiet, "Will the choir please file from the stage, being very careful that you do not trip on your heavenly raiment as you go down the stairs. Go to the seats reserved for you on the left side of the church. Follow the choir leader, Mrs. Morris, who has a flashlight. Sit down quietly. When the choir children have all left the stage will Mary and Joseph, the shepherds, and the wisemen follow. While you do that, let us sing together, 'It Came Upon the Midnight Clear.'"

So everybody sang and it was really pretty. Someone was carrying the manger and some other things off the platform in the dark so I knew they were getting ready for us. When the carol was over, the minister stood up and turned on a flashlight and said, "We hope that the lights can be repaired before you leave, but if they are not, please tell your children to stay close to you and to move carefully in order to avoid accidents. Be particularly cautious on the front steps for they may be icy."

Miss McCarthy guided me out to the center of the stage and had me sit down. She put a flashlight on the table, standing on end, but whispered, "Not yet."

The minister said, "Miss McCarthy's class will conclude our program with a dramatization of a short story by Leo Tolstoi. The name of it is *Adyevich*. The part of the Russian cobbler is played by Wallace Meekin. Carol Bernard is the soldier's wife and Amiella Meekin plays her small daughter. The apple woman is Elizabeth Holbrook and the two little boys are Lonnie and Benjamin Meekin. In the absence of electric power, we will make do with a flashlight. Perhaps, on that day in a far-off Russian city, it was dark in the streets and in the little basement room where Adyevich mended his shoes."

Then Miss McCarthy whispered to me, "Now," and I pushed the button on the flashlight and she began to tell the story. I realized that she was without any light at all and was doing it from memory, and in a way that made it easier. It was just like she was telling us again, "Use *your* words. Do it your own way."

The only thing was, I knew something was wrong. Because when the minister had turned on the flashlight, I got a pretty clear look at the people just in front of him and my aunt was not there any more. There was a vacant place and I knew it was hers because Liz's mother was still there. Nothing that I could think of would keep Aunt Foster Mary from seeing her kids in this play. Well, only one thing, something must have happened to Alonzo.

Miss McCarthy was telling the part about Adyevich seeing the soldier's wife and the little girl and calling them in. I did it, and I said something like, "Have something to eat with me," and then I remember telling the soldier's wife she could take the shawl, but I didn't really get my mind off Alonzo until I saw Amiella, her eyes big and expectant in front of me. She was holding her breath to see what would happen next. I smiled at her and said, "I made a pair of shoes for another child, a long time ago." I reached into my pocket and pulled out a pair of soft little red boots. They were really bedroom slippers but Aunt Foster Mary and I thought they would look like shoes to the audience, and of course, this audience could hardly see a thing. Maybe that was why they were listening so close. Anyway, I think they heard her gasp when I showed her the shoes and said, "I think these would fit you. Wait a minute and I'll finish them." So I pounded and pretended to sew and then she stuck her foot out and I put them on.

She whispered, "Do I get to keep them?" And I said, "Yes."

"Oh," she sighed, leaning down to feel the soft leather. "All my life I've wanted a pair of red shoes."

She hugged me and then they said good-bye and made like they were going up the stairs to the street. I pretended to be watching them, but I was really looking at that still vacant seat in the first row. I had a picture of Alonzo back in that operating room. Maybe his insides had been injured after all, when he fell. Or maybe the leg had become infected. If it didn't get well, would the doctor have to cut it off?

I forgot all about what part came next and I just stood there with my insides hammering and all I wanted to do was to run off that stage and find out where my aunt had gone. I heard the soft, clear voice of Miss McCarthy going on with the story but I had lost track of everything she was saying: the words just didn't make sense to me.

Suddenly Liz came tearing on stage, chasing Lonnie

154

and Bennie. I remembered to stop her and I held her arm, but I whispered, "Where's Auntie? Do you know?" She shook her head, and yelled, "Let me go! Those wicked boys stole my apples!" and she acted like she was trying to pull herself away, but her eyes showed me that she had noticed the empty seat, too.

"Don't worry, Bud," she whispered, so I said, out loud this time, "Can't you forgive them? Haven't *you* ever been hungry?" and she smiled with relief and somehow we went ahead with the play.

Before I knew it we had come to the evening scene. I was sitting beside the little chest, and I didn't have to pretend I was an old man, sad and lonesome. I just thought of Alonzo, away from his family on Christmas Eve. I thought, Just bring him home safe. It don't matter that he can't work for a long time, or even that he might lose his job. Or even that we might have to move. We'll take care of him, just like he's always taken care of us. Only bring him back.

Miss McCarthy's voice stopped and I knew it was time to speak. The words I had learned were not in my head and I couldn't see by that dim light to read so I just put my hand on the Bible and I said, "When I read in this book all about how You used to be here and how You would walk on these roads and talk to all the people, then I think that it would sure have been good to see You and to hear Your voice, Lord. And sometimes when I'm working why I look at all those feet going by in the snowy street . . ." I stopped a minute and looked up and there was the window; it was real, not make-believe. I could look through it ". . . And I think I see a pair of dusty sandals stop outside and I hurry to the door to let You in."

I knew those weren't the right words but they were the best ones I could think of. I forgot what was supposed to happen next. Had we ever practiced the end of the play?

Then from the wing, but sounding close and warm and talking right to me, I heard, "I was with you today, Adyevich."

"Where were You, Lord?" I asked. "I didn't see You."

And the Voice said, "I was with you with the woman and the child. I came to you again with the apple woman and the boys. I was cold and you made Me warm. I was hungry and you fed Me. I was thirsty and you quenched My thirst. Inasmuch as ye did it unto the least of these, My brethren, ye did it even unto Me."

After a few minutes, Mrs. Morris began to play softly, "Silent Night, Holy Night," and the people went down the aisle without talking to each other.

But I just sat there in the dark and I thought, Why, this story really was about people like Alonzo and Foster Mary. People who have room for little kids who don't have any folks or any place to stay. They might not have any home themselves, but somehow they make one: in drafty shacks, in old cars parked beside the river bank, sometimes just around a campfire. Alonzo don't need a hammer and nails to build the kind of walls that keep out fear anymore than Aunt Foster Mary needs a big fancy stove to feed hungry children.

I stood up and tried to see down that dark aisle where all the crowd was going. We're going to be all right, I thought. Auntie isn't afraid of what's going to happen, just so we're together, she and Alonzo and us kids. There ain't nothing going to hurt us, we're safe.

156

Liz was standing there, waiting for me.

"Come on, Bud," she said, "let's go and find Mom. She'll know where your aunt is. I told her I'd meet her outside the front door."

"I got to get the kids," I said. I turned around and there they were, with their hats and coats on, even their mittens.

"Here, Bud, here's yours," said Bennie. I put them on. The boys were very quiet. I wondered if they had noticed anything.

"Amiella, you can't wear those shoes out in the snow," I told her.

"They're boots!"

"Just make-believe boots, hon," I said, so she sighed, and sat on the steps leading down from the platform and took them off. Lonnie helped her put on her brown ones and she clutched the red pair in her hands. I held the flashlight and when they were ready, turned it out and left it on the table.

"O.K., you can carry them. Now, let's get goin'."

We went down the aisle of the church. Ahead of us we could see a gleam of light coming in through the open front door where the minister was standing, shaking hands with people.

"Well, the arc lamp's on outside so the power isn't off," I told Liz. "I guess we blew all the fuses in the church, though. Oh, excuse me," I said as I bumped into somebody. "I wasn't watching. I thought everyone had left."

"Not everybody," said a voice I knew. "Didn't think we'd go home without our kids, did you?" There he was in a wheelchair, grinning his old happy grin, with Aunt Foster Mary beside him, holding his hand. The kids swarmed all over Alonzo.

"I didn't know you were comin'!" cried Amiella, her cheek pressed tight against his. "Uncle 'Lonzo, lookit! See my red shoes!"

"Honey, I seen you get them. I was here all the time." To me he said, "I worked on the doc and he said seein's how my kids were all going to perform tonight I could come home. I got to go in to his office day after tomorrow, though. But I'm through at that danged hospital!"

"Uncle 'Lonzo, I don't think you ought to say 'danged' in church," Lonnie reproved him.

"What's happened to *him*?" Alonzo asked, astonished, and we all laughed.

"Let's go, I can't wait to see my own house and sleep in my own bed and have some good home cookin'." He looked around at us all and his eyes were wet. "I missed you so much."

"Well, just don't go away no more, Uncle 'Lonzo," Amiella said, and he answered, "I sure ain't plannin' on it."

We had pushed him to the door and Auntie was saying, still excitedly, "Mrs. Millhouser got the message and knew we were at the church so she and her boys went after Alonzo and brought him here. We didn't want to make a commotion, your play was just about to start. That's why I came back to sit with him. I was sure you couldn't see that I was gone. He thought I ought not to push the wheelchair down the aisle."

"I was afraid to get any closer. I might have just

climbed right up on that platform to hug each one of you," Alonzo told us. "You are all good actors. I tell you I was proud!"

"You have a right to be proud," Mr. Wilson said, leaning over to shake hands with Uncle. "You have a fine family, Mr. Meekin. They gave us something to remember this Christmas."

He talked to Alonzo and Auntie a few minutes and while he was talking, Miss McCarthy came hurrying out. "Oh, I'm so glad you are still here!" she cried. "One of the cherubs got sick—too much Christmas candy before the performance. Anyway, I've been taking care of her until her mother came." She looked at us. "It turned out fine, didn't it? You are real troupers; lights out and everything, but it didn't faze you a bit. Even the little ones—most kids would have been scared."

"Bud was there," Bennie said, matter-of-fact like he always is.

Miss McCarthy looked at me and smiled. "Yes," she said, "Bud was certainly there." Then she smiled again and waved good-bye to us. "Happy vacation!" she called back. Would you believe it, a teacher, and here I was, feeling sort of sorry that we wouldn't be seeing her until after New Year's.

Mr. Wilson was helping Auntie with the wheelchair. They folded it and put it in the trunk. Liz's mother was in the driver's seat, waiting for us all. We put Alonzo in the back with his right leg up on the seat. Amiella wanted to sit on the floor by him, so we let her. Aunt Foster Mary got in the front with Bennie in the middle and Lonnie on her lap.

"Get in, Bud!" Amiella called.

"Now, how can we?" I asked. "Liz and me—Liz and I will walk. See you in a few minutes."

We watched them drive down the street toward her place and then we started to walk through the quiet town. Our feet slipped in the snow. We moved together and I took hold of her hand. I took off my glove and hers, too, and stuck them in my pocket, and her hand was warm and soft in mine. Neither one of us said a single word all the way there. We just looked up into the sky and saw all the twinkly stars and we smiled at each other. Inside myself I said to her, "They look different tonight," and I wasn't surprised when she answered, "Of course, it's Christmas." We went by the bowling alley and the post office and a little grocery and by and by we came to the motel.

Our folks were talking out in front. They rolled down the car window and we stuck our heads in.

"We won't come in tonight, Esther," Auntie said. "Alonzo's tired and so are the kids."

"Hardly room enough for everybody, anyway," Liz's mother answered. "We didn't get in our new place by Christmas, after all. But we got a nice room picked out and we're movin' next week. So next time you come, we'll have a little party."

I was hoping Aunt Foster Mary could tell what I was thinking, like she usually does, but I didn't need to worry. She would have said it, anyway.

"And tomorrow we'll have one at our house," she told them, smiling, and then looking at all of us, "We'll always remember this year, won't we, kids? The year we had two Christmases. And we got such a lot to celebrate! We couldn't do it without you. So Bud'll be by to pick you up. Will it be all right if he comes early, about ten o'clock?"

They both said yes, that would be fine, and they'd love to come and Liz's mother said, "But we don't want to crowd you."

Auntie cried, "Land! We got a whole orchard to spread out in. If them kids get to celebratin' too loud, we'll send them up on Apricot Hill!"

Mrs. Holbrook got out and I started to slide in the front seat but Liz said, "Wait just a minute, will you?" and she ran inside. She came right back out with something in her arms, hugged up against her.

"Merry Christmas!" she said, reaching in to give it to Amiella.

"Oh, a kitty! He's darling!" Amiella squealed.

"It's not a he, it's a she," said Liz, "so pretty soon you might have hundreds . . ."

The kids chimed in right away, ". . .Of cats, thousands of cats, millions and billions and trillions of cats!"

Liz was gone again. "Good night, Liz! Thank you! I love her!" Amiella called, but I knew she was coming back and she did. This time she had a box.

"What is it?" they all asked, and she said, "This one is for Bud."

He was round and fat and a soft brown color all over, except for his white nose. He whimpered a little bit because of the cold, so she picked him up and I opened my coat in front so she could slide him in next to my sweater.

I wanted to say something, to thank her, but everybody was listening. I just wanted Liz to hear. So I said, in our silent language we were just beginning to learn, "How did you know? How could you ever have known that all my life I've wanted a little dog just like this?"

She smiled up at me and reached in and smoothed his fur. He snuggled up close. I could feel his little heart pounding, keeping time with mine. Then it seemed like Liz answered my thoughts and said, "Apple pickers can't have dogs. First you have to have a house. Then you can have a dog. And everything."

He was asleep in no time, and so were the kids. It was quiet in the car and along our road. We turned in at Ransome's and stopped in front of the cottage.

"I'll get Alonzo," I whispered. "You sit here, Auntie. I'll be back for the kids."

But she got out and stood Lonnie on his feet and he made it up the path. I unlocked the door and put the little dog down next to the stove. Then between us Aunt Foster Mary and I walked Alonzo into the house. Lonnie was sitting on the floor, wide awake now, playing with my puppy. I left them there and went back for the other two kids, but before I woke them I looked up at the sky again. The same stars were shining down, making the roof all silvery and frosted. I walked around to the side of the house and paced along from the front to the back.

"What're you doing, love?" Auntie called from the open door, light spilling out all around her onto the white snow. "Need any help?"

"No, I'm coming," I answered. But first I kicked the ground. Pretty hard now, but spring would come. And this spring I was going to make sure that Aunt Foster Mary got her flower garden.

About the Author

Celia Strang lives in Seattle, Washington, near the apple country of *Foster Mary*. "I'm interested in the life of the day-to-day person," the author says, and she drew upon her experiences with the apple pickers to write this book, her second published novel. Her first, *Eventually on Top of a New Tomorrow*, won first prize in the Pacific Northwest Writer's Conference. The first two chapters of *Foster Mary* were awarded first place in a Seattle short-story contest.

A former schoolteacher, a mother of three, and a grandmother of fifteen, Celia Strang also bowls and plays bridge. A great traveler, she has toured the entire United States by bus because, as she says, "The people I'm interested in ride buses."

Celia Strang is currently at work on several novels.